UNDER THE LONDON SKY

Also by Anna Woltz

Talking to Alaska
My Especially Weird Week with Tess

UNDER THE LONDON SKY

ANNA WOLTZ

Translated by
Michele Hutchison

A Rock the Boat Book

First published by Rock the Boat, an imprint of Oneworld Publications Ltd, 2025
Originally published in Dutch as *De tunnel* by Em. Querido's Uitgeverij, 2021

A CIP record for this title is available from the British Library

ISBN 978-1-83643-061-2
eISBN 978-1-83643-062-9

This publication has been made possible with financial support from the Dutch Foundation for Literature.

Nederlands
letterenfonds
dutch foundation
for literature

Typeset by Geethik Technologies
Printed and bound in Great Britain by Clays Ltd, Elcograf S.p.A

Translation handcrafted without the use of generative AI.

The authorised representative in the EEA is eucomply OÜ,
Pärnu mnt 139b–14, 11317 Tallinn, Estonia
(email: hello@eucompliancepartner.com / phone: +33757690241)

Oneworld Publications Ltd
10 Bloomsbury Street
London WC1B 3SR
England

To my mother

First this

There are three of us now.

At first, we were four, but one of us will die. It's better you know this before we begin.

One of us dies, but that's not all this story is about. Of course that changed everything. But this is also about the three of us who managed to survive.

The three of us went through it all: the bombs, the fires, the nights. We're still alive.

Our lives are only just beginning…

There were four of us, but often we might just as well have been alone.

As you lie in the dark, hard iron girders poking into your back, while night after night the world above your head is smashed apart, what use are other people?

Sometimes none at all.

But other times they help.

The four of us were together and that helped.

1

A boy is standing on the other side of the street. He's leaning against a wall with his hands in his pockets. The sleeves of his old shirt are rolled up, his arms are streaked with grime.

He looks at me.

I'm standing in a queue with two hundred other people and still I'm convinced he's looking at me.

He's too young to be a soldier but too old to be a schoolboy. His trousers are dirty. His brown hair is so long it falls in front of his eyes.

Now he's looking at Robbie, who is right next to me. We act like I'm taking care of my younger brother, but we all know it's the other way round. Robbie is taking care of me.

I spent a year lying in bed, and all that time, Robbie was out in the city. He knows every market stall, every stray dog, every alleyway. No one winces when they see him.

The tall boy across the street whistles. It's a short, bossy note. Robbie looks up and the boy beckons to him.

"Stay here," I whisper. But Robbie had waited a whole year for the war to begin in earnest, and now it's finally here.

Each night bombs fall. All over London you can see massive fires and destroyed houses and sometimes even dead people. And what are we doing? We've been standing in a queue for more than four hours now, with a little cart full of blankets and pillows.

"Don't go to him!" I whisper, but Robbie is already crossing the street.

I stay where I am, all on my own among strangers. I haven't slept in days and it's like the world is made of glass. One wrong move and the whole thing will shatter.

I stand there, frozen to the spot. I wrap my cardigan tightly around my summer dress. My legs are cold. The air smells of soot.

Newspapers aren't allowed to write anything about the air raids. No one wants Hitler reading about the damage they've caused. But if you live within a few miles of the docks, you don't need the news to tell you what's happening. Every evening it's like the sun's setting on the wrong side. The sky to the east glows a fiery orange. We all know the docks are on fire. And you can smell exactly which warehouse is ablaze – shiploads of peppercorns that came halfway around the world before going up in flames. Burning syrup, tea, rum.

On the other side of the street, the boy is pointing at me. Robbie begins to grin, and for a moment the possibility flickers through my mind: is he talking to Robbie about asking me out?

My brother runs back excitedly. He's almost mowed down by a double-decker bus. A fire engine filled with firefighters honks its horn loudly, but Robbie doesn't care.

"Ella, that lad there needs you!"

A silence falls around us and heads turn in our direction. There are only women in the queue, a few children, the odd elderly man with a bent back and missing teeth.

But of course I can't leave the queue – it would mean giving up our place. So Robbie pulls me to one side and I lean in towards him. I've no idea what happens on a date. And my blue dress with the daisies on it is too short. I'd need to alter it first.

"He saw your leg," Robbie says quietly. "And he saw how pale you are and how poorly you look." He gazes up at my face. "I know, sorry. But that's what he said! Should I have punched him?"

I sigh. "No. Go on."

"Well, he's called Jack and he's sixteen. And he's got a plan. If we say to the guard on the door that you really can't wait in the queue this long, we might be given priority. And then they'd let us in straight away and we could be the first to pick a sleeping spot."

I feel dizzy but that's nothing new.

"But I haven't told you the best bit," Robbie whispers. He's beaming, and I wish *I* was nine years old. I wish I could race through the streets and feel the same happiness whenever I spotted a couple of our Spitfires flying over. "Jack says we could earn a lot of money. There are always people who turn up late. They have to work and when they finally get here, there's no room. But if we lay down a few extra blankets, we could earn loads selling those spots."

"Really?" I say. "He wants to charge people for a safe place to sleep?"

Robbie nods. "He did it yesterday – he knows how to. If your leg can get us in early, we'll split the profit. That's what he said!"

I take a deep breath.

The air-raid siren could go off again at any moment. We're all on constant alert. People are putting on a brave face but London feels like a UXB. I learned that term last week. An unexploded bomb.

"Well?" Robbie asks.

I clear my throat. "No."

"But—"

"Out of the question."

Suddenly, there's movement in the queue. The gate to the Underground has opened. Finally, we can go inside.

The flock of people quickly grab their bundles of bedding and pillows, bags containing sandwiches and thermos flasks of tea, prams filled with belongings. Everyone waits their turn, but you can sense they are impatient to storm down the steps, away from the sunlight and open streets, into the depths.

Now I'll have to hobble the entire stretch to the entrance knowing that Jack is still looking at us. My body is stiff from queuing for hours. I feel the pressure of the people behind me.

I start to walk.

My left leg is slower than the right; I drag my foot with every step I take. The doctors said I was incredibly lucky. I don't need crutches or a brace, just special shoes.

UXB, I think to myself, as if it was a swear word.

How incredibly lucky!

I'm fourteen now. How many pairs of special shoes will that add up to?

Robbie is walking beside me, pushing the cart with our belongings. Everything about him seems indignant. His coarse, spiky hair, his grazed knees, his shorts held up by braces.

"It's so unfair!" He sticks out his chin. "I've almost saved enough money for a new plane. Jack said he earned seven shillings yesterday. That's loads of money!"

I grab his arm.

"Don't you understand?" I whisper.

"I understand more than you do," he whispers back immediately.

I shake my head. "If we lose the war, it will be because of cheats like Jack. Think about it! People who've worked hard all day – you're going to make them pay for a safe place to shelter? While a fella like him just loafs about all day!"

"Why doesn't he work then?"

"Well, exactly," I say. "That's my point."

Before we enter Liverpool Street station, I take another look around me. I see the black cabs, and the groups of soldiers, and the pub with sandbags in front of it. It's four in the afternoon. We won't go outside again until the morning. I've no idea whether the city will still be standing then.

Suddenly, I hear a cheerful voice behind me. "Shall I give you a hand with that cart?"

I turn round.

It's Jack.

2

He's a head taller than me. His arms are muscular and his eyes are the same colour as the barrage balloons, the silvery giants above our heads. They fill London's skies, tied to the ground with heavy cables.

All summer we'd gazed up happily at the massive balloons. It felt like every neighbourhood had its own pet. The obedient creatures in the sky would protect us from aeroplanes.

But the new bombers fly higher than the highest balloons.

"Leave us alone," I say to Jack.

The people behind us push forward. There are at least a hundred of them, and they can't see that we've stopped here. I look at the steep steps and realise I can't help Robbie with the cart. And except for Jack, everyone has their hands full.

Each family sends a scout out ahead: an elderly grandad or aunt, or a girl with a bad leg like me who has nothing better to do. The rest follow later.

"*How kind of you,*" Jack says as he takes the front of the cart. "That's what you say when someone tries to help you."

There's a trace of dried blood on his cheek. He grins at me. He hasn't spent a second in the queue and he's still getting into the station. Nobody says anything because he's helping a poor wretch and her little brother.

I clench my teeth and make my way down the stairs, step by step. I hope Jack doesn't look back, and at the same time I tell myself that's ridiculous. Why should I care if he sees my face? What does it matter if he knows I'm in pain?

Below ground, there are long queues of people in front of the ticket machines and the ticket booths. It doesn't matter whether you're travelling to another tube stop or spending the night down there: no one gets through without a ticket.

I stumble and Robbie gestures at a narrow bench next to the wall. "You can go and sit down. I'll buy the tickets."

It's strange, I know, but after all those months in bed it feels as though the world is turning faster than it used to. People move quicker, the light is brighter, sounds are shriller. I sit down on the bench and look at my hands. I'm still in black and white and the world is suddenly in colour.

I rest my head against the wall, exhausted. The sound of explosions replays in my mind.

Last night, Robbie and I spent ten hours hiding in the cupboard under the stairs. Mum didn't fit. She sat on the floor in front of the cupboard door and refused to swap places with me.

We didn't say a word for hours. Anti-aircraft fire popped all around us, planes roared, dull explosions resounded through the city.

And then there was that bomb. A shrieking whistle came straight towards us, and I knew for sure: this was it.

Then I thought: *Who cares. Come on then, stupid bomb!*

But the bomb wasn't for us. It landed two streets away. And the children squashed up inside the cupboard under the stairs, like us, were pulled out of the rubble today, dead.

So that's why we're here.

When Robbie returns with the tickets, we head to the escalators. Jack has abandoned us, so I don't have to pretend I'm bravely bearing my tragic fate any more. We can manage fine without him now. On the escalator, I use one hand to stay the cart and the other to clasp the handrail.

I stare at the posters that slowly pass by on the wall beside me. A photo of two rosy-cheeked children with a warning underneath: ***Children are safer in the countryside… Leave them there***. An advert for a headache tonic. A poster urging people to grow their own vegetables.

And then I make the mistake of looking into the depths.

It's like a scene from a nightmare. Without moving a muscle, we glide down a giant tunnel into the belly of the earth, a world of zooming metal and electric light. The last time I was here was a year ago. After leaving the hospital, I didn't dare venture here and now I remember why.

At the bottom of the escalator, the crowds push us further into the white-tiled tunnels. We turn a corner, then another, until we reach the long, narrow platform of the Central Line. The rails charged with electricity run alongside us. If you tumbled on to them, you'd be fried.

"Look!" Robbie's tone is excited, as though we're on a Sunday outing. "There's still a space free next to the wall."

He runs towards it and pulls out the bedding from the cart. "Dad can go here, Mum here and me here. Uncle and Aunty can go there… Where do you want to go?"

I clench my fists.

For a whole year I've done stupid exercises and bitten my cheeks to pieces every time hot compresses were laid on my body. The plan was to come out the other end ready for adulthood. I'd look for a job, I'd secretly write stories, I'd bake war cakes with my friends.

A hot and stuffy platform packed with strangers who've brought along half of their belongings *wasn't* my plan. Sleeping right next to my whole family each night wasn't the plan either.

But I don't have a choice. I sit down and stretch out my skinny legs on the blanket. A platform attendant shouts sternly that we need to leave space for tube passengers. The trains will still be running for hours.

Perched next to me, Robbie devours an egg sandwich made with margarine. Suddenly, he starts waving. Five blankets away, a dusty boy waves back.

"He goes to our school," Robbie says with his mouth full. He gets up. "I'm off to see him, Ella."

The school's been closed for a year already and I'm not even a pupil any more, but he calls it "our school" all the same.

"Be back by six," I tell him. "That's when the others are coming. And you have to stay on the platform!"

He doesn't look back and I slowly exhale.

I grab the notebook I hid at the bottom of the cart this morning. My mother says I need to stop making up stories. What good are words if you can darn a sock instead?

But I want to get out of here. The notebook in my hands is a ladder. It's a rope of sheets knotted together, a hot-air balloon.

The smell of mothballs rises from the bedding around me. I don't want to hear tube trains thundering through dark tunnels. I don't want to be stared at by passengers who have to weave their way around the hordes of people camped out on the platform, all hiding from the bombs that will fall tonight.

I don't want to look at every man who goes past to see if he's Jack.

I take my pencil and begin to write.

3

I thought I disliked my own body, but that first night in the Underground, I come to the conclusion that other people's bodies are even worse.

Here we lie, three hundred strangers on a brightly lit platform. It always smells musty but after so many hours with so many people there, it's horrendous. A suffocating mixture of stale smoke, sweat and pee.

We lie side by side like skinny sardines in a massive tin. Our heads are close to the wall; our feet point at the tracks. The people who arrive last are the unluckiest: they have to lie sideways where all the feet are.

I've got a flowery bedspread over me and a rolled-up cardigan under my head. Close by, a toddler is being put to bed in an open suitcase; a little further away, a newborn baby is being nursed by its mother. She sits in the middle of the platform, a breast half bared, but nobody complains.

The trains stop running at half past ten but even after that, there isn't a moment's peace and quiet. People cough and turn, sniff and clear their throats. They itch with such a frenzy that after a while I'm sure I'm covered in fleas too.

And then there's my family.

I didn't notice my mother until a shadow fell over my notebook. She licked her finger, leaned in and cleaned something from my cheek. I silently closed my notebook and picked up the stocking that still needed to be darned.

And now they're lying around me. My giant of an uncle who is always happy, my shy aunt who never says a word. My father, who looks grey with exhaustion even when he's asleep.

Ever since the bombing began, he's worked every night as an ARP warden. ARP stands for "air raid precautions". He patrols the streets while everyone else takes shelter. He checks that there are no chinks of light coming through any windows; he puts out incendiary bombs; he's the first to arrive at houses that are hit.

It should feel so safe, the city filled with wardens walking around at night. Except that it's my own father out there when the bombs fall. This is his only night off; tomorrow he will be out there again.

Robbie is sleeping next to me with his knees pulled up, his spiky blond hair shining in the glaring light. At home we share a bedroom, and I thought he put up with me the same way he puts up with so much stuff: lice, holes in his shoes, lumpy porridge, a big sister in his bedroom.

But without saying a word, he came to lie down next to me.

*

I don't sleep a wink that first night.

Bombs fall above ground while the tunnels below ground echo with snores. Just after midnight two people begin to kiss. I can clearly hear the noise they make and even though I don't want to, I keep on listening. I feel a tingling in my lips, which makes me furious because I know I'll never be kissed.

At ten to two in the morning, an old man pees on the rails. Not quietly in a corner, but right under the big station clock. My forehead is clammy with sweat, my eyes burn. I want to scream but of course I don't. Screaming wastes too much oxygen: I learned that in the hospital.

And then, at quarter past three, I see Jack.

He walks towards me along the narrow strip of the platform that is kept clear. His hair is sticking up all over the place. Sometimes he has to step over an arm or a leg; once, he bends down to cover a little girl's shoulders with her blanket.

And then he sees me and stops.

He's just covered up that little girl, and for a second I have this crazy hope that he's watching me more closely than the rest of them.

That he can see who I used to be.

That he can see me in colour.

He slowly takes something out of his pocket, and I hold my breath. I don't know what I'm expecting. A ladder? A rope of sheets knotted together? A hot-air balloon?

They are shiny coins. He holds them up triumphantly and gives me that same smile he did at the top of the station steps. The smile that says, *I can get away with anything.*

So he did it again. Made ordinary people pay for a safe place to sleep. I want to say something or give him a scornful look at least, but he walks on.

His footsteps echo off the bare, curved ceiling. And then it happens. He turns his left foot inwards and pretends to walk with a limp.

He whistles as he disappears into a corridor. I sit there in total silence.

*

When we exit Liverpool Street station, I can finally breathe again.

The platform attendants sent us packing as soon as the all-clear was sounded. Now they're quickly scrubbing the station clean before the tubes start running.

It's like I'm seeing London for the first time. It's quarter past six in the morning and dawn is breaking.

The sky is grey velvet; the bombers are gone. The anti-aircraft fire has stopped. People trudge home through the silent streets with their bundles and carts. Anyone who doesn't have to start work straight away goes back to bed for a little extra sleep.

It's a ten-minute walk to our house from the station. We're getting used to the faint smell of burning. We pay no attention to the clouds of dust in the distance. Now we sniff the air for fresh fires, scan for suffocating billows of smoke, listen out for sirens in the neighbourhood.

The closer we get to our own street, the faster we walk. Until we turn the final corner.

It's still standing. We still have a house.

4

I wake up hours later in a quiet house. Straight away I spot a note beside the bed.

My mother is already back in the queue for the station. I need to swap places with her at half past two so she can go off to a Women's Voluntary Service meeting.

She can finally attend one again.

When I came out of hospital, my mother took care of me for months. No one dared to visit. The doctors said I wasn't infectious any more, but what do doctors know? Maybe there was something bad floating about my room. Maybe it was better not to breathe my air into your lungs.

For months I saw only my parents and Robbie. I read everything in the library. I wrote stories in my notebook. In the early days I missed my friends, but later I didn't.

I wash my face and hands in the kitchen sink, eat leftover cold porridge from the saucepan and stuff my notebook into my cardigan pocket. Then I go outside. It's cloudy and windy. Autumn is coming.

Before I reach the entrance to the Tube, I have to pass the overground station. A line of small children are on their way to catch a train, swinging their teddy bears, suitcases and gas masks excitedly as they go.

A group of young soldiers can't stop laughing, a woman pushes a rattling cart filled with apples, the paperboy shouts, "Read all about the king's radio broadcast! New medals for war heroes!"

And then someone stops in front of me.

"Excuse me, sorry to bother you."

The first thing I notice is her legs. She's not wearing a skirt or a dress, but a brown pair of men's trousers cinched in with a belt. The trouser legs are rolled up so she can't trip over them.

From the waist upwards the girl looks like a film star. She's wearing a pale blue blouse, she has dark curls and a little hat perched sideways on her head. On her arm she has a bag that is so stuffed it looks like she's just robbed a bank.

"I'm looking for a hospital," she says. "Could you point me in the right direction?"

She talks like people on the radio do. I've never heard anyone speak like that in real life. I quickly brush a strand of hair out of my face.

"Do you need a doctor? If you turn left at the corner…"

She begins to laugh. "Today is the one day I don't need a doctor. My sisters find it highly amusing that I'm never ill and yet the doctor has to be called out for me more than anyone else. In fifteen years, I've fallen off three horses, nearly drowned in a home-made boat, tumbled from the roof twice and been bitten by a moody rat. Sorry, where's the hospital?"

I can't keep my eyes off her. She looks totally different from the tired, grey people around us. This girl doesn't look like she's bravely ploughing on. She seems genuinely excited about the day ahead.

"There's the London Hospital in Whitechapel," I say. I feel more excited about the day ahead now too. "It's a half-hour walk." I point eastwards.

"Aha," the girl says. "That way. Thank you." She doesn't move.

I see her looking down Artillery Lane. The street bends almost immediately, and alleys behind it are even narrower and cross each other at funny angles. She'll get completely lost.

I hesitate.

My mother's still waiting in the queue. She's counting on me to relieve her. If I don't go, she won't be able to attend her meeting.

And still I say to the girl, "I'll come with you."

"How kind of you! But…" She looks at my leg. "Isn't it too far for you?"

"No," I say bluntly.

She carries on staring at my leg. "Were you born that way?"

"A year ago I could run faster than all three of the greengrocer's lads."

"Might it still get better?"

"No. No more races for me."

"I'm sorry," she says in a serious tone. She holds out her hand. "I'm Quinn."

I pretend not to see her hand. For months nobody wanted to touch me. Now I've forgotten how it works.

"I'm Ella."

We set off down Artillery Lane. When Quinn walks, it's like the pavement is made of rubber. Or she's made of the newest kind of elastic. Passers-by stare at her trousers and a skinny, barefooted boy shouts out something about "a fella with knockers", but Quinn just gives him a friendly wave.

"I thought a pair of trousers would be essential in the war," she says to me. "The stable boy lent me these, so they smell of straw and horse sweat, but if a bomb drops, nobody will be able to complain about my skirt lifting up."

She looks around. "Why isn't anything damaged here? It wasn't all propaganda on the radio, was it? If there aren't any bombs, I might as well have stayed at home."

"Really?" I ask. "You've come to see the bombs?"

"Do you think that's mad?" she replies calmly. "Of course I'd rather there weren't any bombs. But if there are, I want to be here."

We walk along an ancient alleyway so tight that cars and horse-drawn carts can't fit. The shops have colourful fronts, signs with gold lettering swing above our heads.

"How delightfully picturesque!" Quinn cries enthusiastically. "The peeling paint and that tailless cat and those smelly slop buckets…"

"Welcome to the posh part of the neighbourhood," I say.

"How old are these houses then?" Quinn asks after a pause. "Might they be Georgian?"

I really have no idea. I'm out of breath and every step I take is a step further away from my mother.

She's going to be furious. And terribly worried. I know this and still I carry on walking.

She has to learn that she can't keep stuffing me into a cupboard under the stairs, I tell myself. She has to learn that I'm not a child any more.

I just need to work out what I am now.

At my side, Quinn is still acting like she's Princess Elizabeth seeing a normal street for the first time in her life. "Oh, just look at that teeny-tiny little house! And those crooked shutters…"

And then she's silent.

There's nothing quaint about the next street. Just a great big hole.

An entire terraced house has gone completely. The front of the house next to it has been ripped away. You can see inside all the rooms: on the first floor, a wrought-iron bed is balancing on the edge while stockings hang to dry on a collapsed clothes horse.

The street is filled with bricks, splintered beams and dust. Men wearing helmets are clearing away rubble. Further up the street, two women are sweeping up glass.

A man holds hands with two little girls and stares at the gap in the row of houses. His clothes are torn, his hair is covered in plaster dust. The girls are crying.

That's what it looks like then: a family with a hole in it.

"It wasn't propaganda," Quinn says quietly. "Bombs really are falling."

I glance at her and see that there are tears in her eyes.

"Those bloody bastards." She balls her fists. "If I was a boy, I'd join the army right now!"

"But you're only fifteen, aren't you?"

"What does that matter? I don't have a todger – that's the biggest problem for them."

I gawp at her.

"I don't get it at all," Quinn says. "The whole world revolves around whether or not you've got a todger. If you've got one, they give you a gun and you can shoot down the rest of them. If you don't have one, you have to stay at home and wait. That's hardly an efficient way of winning a war, is it?"

I'm still gawping, and she begins to giggle. "Sorry. Does it bother you, me going on about private parts in the middle of the street?"

"It's uh..." I try to imitate her plummy voice. "It's *a little* awkward."

"I've got three older sisters who discuss absolutely everything," Quinn says, "and I read a lot."

"I read too," I say, somewhat breathlessly. "But different books from you."

"Come on," she says, making a beeline through the dust and shards of glass. "We're off to the hospital. At least I can do something there. Tomorrow I'll start work as a nurse."

"But you're fifteen!"

"So what? My governess told me exactly what to expect. You begin with the dirty jobs, of course. But you do get to live all together in a splendid nurses' home. I'm going to sign up now, and I'll pick up my suitcase later."

"But..." I stop.

I don't get it. Just now, at the station, she didn't ask about the London Hospital. She just asked for the nearest hospital.

"Do they know you're coming?"

"No," she says cheerfully. "But I'm going there now to tell them, you see. There's a war on. I'm ready to empty chamber pots and clean wounds and tell off sobbing soldiers." She looks at me. "Will you wait for me? We'll get a taxi back afterwards. Then you won't have to walk all the way and I can pick up my suitcase. I left it with a young man who looked like he'd just survived a terrible air raid. There was even a streak of blood on his cheek."

I stop. "What?!"

"It was so handy! I got off the train with my heavy suitcase and the boy appeared immediately. The left luggage at the station was completely full, he said. But he knew another place to store my belongings."

"And you believed him?" I ask indignantly. "I know that boy. He's nothing but a crook!"

She sighs. "I was a little afraid that might be the case. Well, luckily, I'm not that attached to the dresses I brought with me." She begins to giggle. "It was a moment of weakness. He was unbelievably charming. My life would be a mess if all the chaps were that handsome."

5

I perch on a low wall, waiting for Quinn to come out of the hospital. Across the street two scruffy-looking dogs are growling at each other. I'm cold and I know my mother's getting really worried as she waits for me in the queue.

But I'm not going back yet.

For the first time in months, I feel like I'm more than just a gammy leg. More than a pale girl who needs a minder all the time. A grey-painted ambulance races by and I straighten my shoulders.

For the first time in months, life is starting to feel a little interesting.

I spot Quinn in the distance, coming back. She walks fast, her curls waving in the wind. And then she's in front of me, her cheeks red, her eyes glittering.

"Those idiots," she cries angrily. "They said I was too young. I'm not allowed to be a nurse. It doesn't matter that I want to work hard, it doesn't matter that there's a war on. The rules are the rules. I should have just brought Violet's ID. People are always saying how alike we look. I could pass for nineteen, couldn't I?"

A taxi approaches and she quickly puts two fingers in her mouth and produces a deafening whistle.

"Learned that from the stable boy," she says proudly. "Come on!"

She pulls me towards the taxi. The driver opens the rear door for us and doesn't blink an eye at Quinn's trousers or my crooked leg.

"Would you really dare do that?" I whisper, as though it's the most normal thing in the world to be riding in a taxi. "Dare to say you're nineteen? Pretend to be someone else?"

"There's nothing I wouldn't dare."

"Really?"

As the taxi takes a detour to avoid some streets that have been closed due to a UXB, Quinn thinks about this.

"I'd do anything *scary*," she says eventually. "The most terrifying things, things other people daren't do. But what I *wouldn't* dare do is get married, have four children and spend my life gardening and drinking tea."

She pauses as we drive past some dust-covered people standing dazedly on a street corner.

"If you're poor, you don't have a garden," I say with a shrug. "And if you're an invalid, nobody wants to marry you. The drinking tea part is the trickiest. Nobody can avoid that."

She gives me a surprised look. And then she begins to giggle.

"You think I'm horribly privileged."

"I don't even know what that is!"

"Sorry, you think I'm a spoiled brat. Spoiled rotten and blind to other people's problems." Without waiting for me to reply, she goes on. "I've no idea where I'll sleep tonight but I'm not going home! I've had it up to here with being Lady Quinn on her country estate, I want—"

"Really?" I interrupt. "You're a lady?"

She sighs. "My father's a lord, I can't do much about it." She gives me a threatening look. "Don't you dare tell anyone! I'm just Quinn here."

"Have you run away from home?"

"Of course I've run away from home! Do you think Mama and Papa would let their youngest daughter go to London on her own? Dressed in a pair of trousers borrowed from the stable boy who's caused so many problems, and carrying a bag filled with jewellery? And planning to become a nurse?" She shakes her head. "Poor Mama and Papa. They've already lost their only son and now I've left too. They shouldn't have been so archaic and authoritarian."

"Sorry, what?" I say.

"Oh!" Quinn begins to laugh. "My governess made me learn three new words from the dictionary each day. They dance around my head and sometimes they just need to get out…"

The taxi stops at the station. She pays the driver with a casual gesture and then we're out on the wet pavement. A fine drizzle is making the cobbles shine.

"So you need somewhere to sleep tonight?" I say.

She looks around. "Yes. I'll try to retrieve my suitcase and then I'll get a taxi to the Savoy. I always stay there with Mama when we come to town. They must have a nice air-raid shelter."

"Or you could come with me," I say. "I'm sleeping in the Underground tonight."

"In the Underground?" She begins to laugh. "What a funny name. I don't know that hotel. Is it good? Do you think they'll have a room for me?"

I'm exhausted – from the walk, from the past nights, from the conversations with a person who uses words I haven't even seen in books. But at the same time, I feel something tingling. "It's not a hotel," I say. "It's just the Underground. Last night I slept on the Central Line platform. Along with a few hundred other people."

"Surely you can't sleep there?" Quinn says in shock. "A platform is hard! And are all those people quiet at night? Are there screens between them or do they just lie next to each other? Does everyone behave decently?"

I shake my head. "No, they don't. I didn't sleep a wink."

"That sounds dreadful," Quinn says. She stands there on the pavement, beaming in the drizzle. "Can I please come too?"

6

"Are you sure this is the right place?" I whisper.

Quinn nods. "The young man pointed to this row of houses. Number forty-three."

She pushes at an unpainted door which is already ajar, and we cautiously go in. The dark corridor smells of cooked cabbage and there's rubbish everywhere: a broken chair, empty bottles, a birdcage, worn-out boots, rusty tin cans.

"Fascinating," Quinn whispers.

"You find this corridor fascinating?"

She giggles. "Yes. Refreshing. I'm used to corridors where you trip over suits of armour and oil paintings."

I hear a rustling to my right, and then my foot brushes against something that feels soft and alive.

"I expect Jack's sold your clothes by now," I whisper, hurrying on.

"Oh, probably." Quinn pats her bulging handbag with satisfaction. "Luckily, the jewellery's in here."

She pounds on the next door, and I hold my breath. I last saw Jack thirteen hours ago. He was whistling as he made his way along the sleeping platform, pretending to walk with a limp.

I hate him. And yet I'm not sure I'll be relieved if he isn't here.

"Come in," calls a husky voice.

Quinn opens the door, and I blink. The gloomy, low-ceilinged room is filled with gigantic piles of bedclothes, pillows and bags. Blue smoke rings coil upwards. An old man is huddled in a chair in the middle of all the baggage. He sucks on a thin cigar and coughs.

"Good afternoon, sir," Quinn says politely. I can tell from her voice that this is a jolly adventure to her. "I've reason to believe a young man brought my suitcase here. Might you know something about it?"

The man wheezes. "Take a look around, young lady. I'm just sitting here."

Quinn gives me a quick glance, and I can see it in her face now too: her eyes are sparkling. Without disturbing the bedclothes, we begin to search the musty maze.

And then I hear a voice behind me.

"Your case is on the left in that corner."

I turn round.

He's there in the doorway. My body tenses but he doesn't look at me. He's looking at Quinn.

His hair falls over his face, the graze on his cheek has become darker. Without wanting to, I hear Quinn's voice inside my head. *My life would be a mess if all the chaps were that handsome.*

"Heavens," Quinn says in surprise. She pushes aside a couple of heavy bags. "That really is my case! You didn't fancy selling it then?"

Jack starts to laugh. "Oh, I did. But it's full of flowery dresses and old books. Load of rubbish."

"So you put everything back in again?" Quinn asks amicably.

"Yes." He pushes back his hair. "I was hoping to find diamonds. That's what I was expecting. But I'm not about to abandon my business here for a heap of skirts."

"What is this place?" Quinn asks as she looks around. Of course she's never been surrounded by so much poor people's stuff in her life before, but she still seems at ease.

Jack grins. "Every day, people have to lug their bedding around. From their houses to the station and back. Now they can leave it here for a few pennies. And before they go back to the shelter, they pick it up again. Old William here gets a couple of cigars for the trouble."

Jack turns to me suddenly. "Nice bit of biz, eh?"

Up to now he's been looking at Quinn. Her body is in his mind. Now he's looking at me and the difference hurts: everything about her is just right, and nothing about me is.

I shrug. "Whatever. Looking after people's bedding is better than hogging sleeping places."

"Don't you worry," he laughs. "I'm still selling sleeping spots. Earns more."

"Until someone tells a copper," I say quietly.

"A copper? I hope not for your sake. They'd go after my assistant."

He waits. Clouds of smoke gather above our heads.

"Your assistant?" I ask, my heart pounding.

"Yeah, funny lad, he is. Don't mind working for scum like me at all. Right now, he's looking after seven of the best sleeping spots. He'll be able to buy a new toy plane soon. That's if no one sends the coppers after him. Mind you, he's a fast runner..."

There's a moment of silence in the room.

And then I call him a word I have never used before.

I turn round. I couldn't care less about Quinn and her suitcase any more; I need to find Robbie. Now.

The whole of London is a UXB, about to explode. People are holding in their emotions. They wait silently in line, keeping a stiff upper lip as the city goes up in flames. But they're longing to let rip, just for a moment. When they discover that Robbie has been hogging spots in the Underground, the whole platform's going to go after him.

As fast as I can, I hobble back down the dark corridor, out of the shabby door, along the shining streets towards the tube entrance. Swear words I didn't even dare think before are echoing around my head.

All those months in bed trying to picture a new life. And now, after a few hours with Quinn and Jack, I'm astonished by myself. I've let my mother down and I'm thinking words a girl of fourteen shouldn't even know.

Who on earth am I?

7

Running away is not something I can do. They catch up with me long before I reach the Underground. Quinn walks to my left with her heavy case, Jack to my right.

"I'll help you," Quinn whispers.

"If you grass on me," Jack says, "you won't be able to walk at all after."

I shudder but Quinn shakes her head in annoyance.

"Jack," she reprimands him, "shut up about Ella's leg. It's rude and it's boring. We know she has a limp. She's hobbling rather obviously between us. It's not like any of us will forget."

I'm concentrating too hard on the approaching steps to say anything.

It's past four and the Underground gates are open to shelterers: we can go straight in. Quinn and Jack follow me in silence, watching as I hobble "rather obviously" down the steep steps.

And then I'm standing at the ticket machines with my coins.

I look at the buttons and don't know what to do. I'm fourteen, but I've completely forgotten how the machines work.

"I'll do it," says Jack without looking at me. He takes the pennies from my freezing hand and chucks them into the slot.

We walk towards the escalator, and I feel dizzy. I'm not just on my way to Robbie but also my mother.

What am I going to say to her? That she looked after me for months but I was too much of an awful person to come and relieve her today? That Robbie's about to go to prison and that we're going to have to squeeze a "lady" into our crowded row of sardines?

Even in the draughty passageways, people are already setting up camp.

"Look at that," Quinn whispers. She looks as though she's visiting the zoo. "Are they really going to sleep here? On the ground, like tramps?"

Jack suddenly stops. He turns round. There are dark rings under his eyes; his jaw is clearly defined.

"Are you from another planet?"

"From a small village," Quinn begins. "Or just outside of one actually. It's…"

But he's not listening. "Tonnes of explosives fall from the sky each night." His voice echoes along the bare walls. "The government didn't give a toss about us. They didn't build enough shelters, and when the air raids began, they kept the Underground closed! We weren't allowed into the one safe place in London. But we refused to let them kill us."

The whole corridor is silent. Jack balls his fists, and for the first time I wonder where he actually lives. He's as poor as a mouse, that's clear. Does he have a house in the East End, where most of the bombs have fallen and where large areas have gone up in flames? Maybe he doesn't even have a home any more.

"The crowds stormed the gates at this station," he says proudly. "We just forced our way in. And now people all over London can shelter in the Underground. The tunnels are ours! So anyone who can't sleep without a mattress –" he gives Quinn a piercing look – "can bugger off."

"Hear, hear," a man lying on the ground says.

We continue through the station in total silence, taking care not to step on people. Quinn drags her huge case unassisted. She pants but I can't help her. And Jack acts as though he hasn't noticed.

The Central Line platform comes closer, and I still have no idea what I'm going to say to my mother. But once we're finally there, Jack doesn't turn right in the direction of my family. He turns left, saying, "He's this way." And we follow.

All around, I hear excited whispers about Quinn in her men's trousers. The people have no idea her bag's full of jewels, but they can tell that she doesn't belong here. Her cheeks are rosy, her shiny blouse fits her perfectly and she looks as though life's an adventure to her.

But that's not how things work. If your life really *is* an adventure – if you're not even sure you'll have a home by tomorrow – you don't look like that.

Jack keeps on walking right to the end of the platform. And then he jumps off it.

"Are you crazy?" I shout. "Watch out for the rails!"

But he grins and strolls into the half-darkness of the tunnel.

"Step over them. They go off into a siding," he shouts back. "The rest of the tunnel's clear. They're extending the Central Line, but work stopped months ago."

I stand there on the very tip of the platform and, peering into the tunnel, understand two things at once.

Jack was right: deep in there are absolutely the best sleeping spots in the whole station. There aren't any tube trains rushing past, it's wonderfully dim, and fewer people walk past than on the platform.

But something else strikes me.

I'll never dare go into this tunnel. Not after the other tunnel.

The feeling comes back to me. The stiff rubber around my neck, the pressure on my ribcage. I hear the machine wheezing as it labours away; I see the mirror above my head. Every day the hands of nurses coming in through hatches on the sides. Every day waiting to see if I'll still be able to feel the touch of their fingers.

I stand on the platform and it's back: a giant *nothing* in the place of my body.

I faint.

8

It's not exactly pleasant, coming to and immediately having to answer a hundred questions. My mother, uncle and aunt are panting in my face, wanting to know if I'm ill, where I was all this time and how I feel now.

I have no idea.

I lie on the platform with the flowery bedspread over me and all I can see is my family. Where's Quinn? Wasn't she going to sleep with us? And where's Jack?

"Here, drink up." Mum supports my head and pours lukewarm tea with a lot of milk and sugar into my mouth. I haven't tasted anything that sweet since sugar got rationed.

"I looked for you everywhere," she whispers. "The other women kept my place in the queue so I could go home and look for you. I looked on the street and in the park and I went to the police station… Where *were* you?"

I don't reply. I want to wrap my arms around her but I don't move. On the blankets either side of us, people are straining their necks so as not to miss any part of our conversation.

"Are you ill?" she asks gently. "Should we call a doctor?"

"I didn't eat enough," I say hoarsely. "That's all."

She shakes her head with a sigh and gets up. As she goes over to our basket of food, Robbie slips into the spot next to me.

"Jack came to get me," he whispers excitedly. "I was waiting in the tunnel and then he said you'd passed out! I had to show them the way to Mum, and then they carried you!"

"Carried me?" I'm still a little light-headed. "Who did?"

"Jack and the trouser lady!"

"Her name's Quinn."

"Really? That's a funny name. Well, Jack grabbed you under your arms and Quinn took your legs. They whisked you up like that and now the whole platform's seen your knickers."

I close my eyes for a moment and can't help picturing it. Quinn lifting up my legs: the normal right leg and the left leg with the special shoe. Jack standing over my head and bending down to lift me by my…

"What's up with Quinn?" Robbie whispers. "We were halfway here when a copper appeared on the platform. You should have seen how fast she vanished! She dropped your legs just like that and scarpered!"

"She ran away when she saw a policeman?"

"Yes. Leaving you to crash to the ground. Or almost. Luckily, Jack had a hold of you. That lad is amazingly strong. He carried you along the platform on his own. He said—"

"Robbie!" My mother's back. "Leave Ella alone."

She sits down next to me and gives me a mashed bean sandwich and another large mug of tea.

I begin to eat in silence. The beans have a sickly taste and stick to the back of my throat. There's no sugar in the tea this time.

"I had to help a girl," I mumble. "She was all on her own and didn't know her way around London."

My mother sighs. "I really needed to go to that meeting. Thousands of people have lost their homes. We have to arrange places for them to stay, food, clothes, bedding."

I take another sticky bite. Another bitter sip.

"I'm sorry," I whisper. "I meant to get here at half past two."

I lie down with my head in her lap. She gently strokes my hair, and I close my eyes.

A year ago, I was even more helpless than a baby. Now I can breathe again. But how do I do the rest?

*

I wake up in the middle of the night. My leg is stiff. I'm cold and hot at the same time. I sit up sleepily. It's ten past midnight according to the platform clock.

I think about my father walking through the blacked-out streets, a steel helmet on his head, a whistle in his pocket, waiting for the next plane. Every morning, when he returns home exhausted, we act like it's normal for him to have survived another night.

And then I think about Quinn. Where is she now? Did she find a safe place to sleep? I rub my eyes; my head is foggy. I sleepily reach for my notebook. Suddenly, I'm wide awake.

My pocket is empty. My book of stories has gone.

It feels like I'm falling. And believe me, I know what that feels like.

It doesn't take long to realise when I must have lost it. Of course, it fell from my pocket when I fainted. Or just after, when they carried me, unconscious, along the platform.

The inside of my mind is lying there somewhere on the grey slabs of the platform.

I cautiously get to my feet; my leg is tingling. I step over Robbie, teeter a little as I climb over my mother, and then make my way towards the tunnel.

Here and there, a few people are still awake, but they pay me no attention. They're used to passers-by; at the end of the platform, there's a folding screen with a stinking slop bucket behind it.

My eyes search the floor. My notebook has a dark blue cover. It won't be very noticeable on the grey stone surface. I check the tracks below, the gap between the rails. Maybe someone kicked it away.

Or maybe someone is reading it right now.

I feel my cheeks burn red even though no one's looking at me.

If it was just a diary, I wouldn't care. My whole life has been insignificant.

But the stories are an improved version. A version where every doctor in that awful hospital was breathtakingly handsome. Where bouquets of flowers and fruit baskets were delivered to the sick girl every day. A version where the world cheered when she got better again.

And there's the bit about the kiss.

Five paragraphs about a young doctor with shiny blond hair and gentle hands. A hero who can't help himself and, one quiet evening, kisses the sick girl passionately, ignoring all the risks of infection.

Idiotic, of course.

And I grew breathless as I wrote it.

Really, I don't know what's wrong with me. But if anyone ever reads those pages, there's only one thing for it – I'll have to send myself into quarantine and never come out.

I've almost reached the end of the platform, the tunnel is getting closer. The stench from the slop bucket is too much. This is where I fainted. But my notebook isn't here.

And then I realise that Quinn might have found it. Or Jack.

I pause, my head reeling. I've no idea where Quinn is now. But I do know where Jack is. Maybe he's taken my idiotic fantasies with him. Into the tunnel.

Now I've allowed that thought to take hold, there's nothing else for it; if Jack's got my book of stories, I have to get it back as fast as possible. I have to go into the tunnel.

My body starts shaking before I've even taken a single step. It's much darker in there than out here. I see three small bulbs hanging down at quite a distance from each other. That's all.

I carefully lower myself down from the platform and step over the dangerous rails. A few hours ago, I was sure I'd never set foot in here. And now I have to because I was mad enough to invent a life when I should have been darning.

My ears are ringing. I peer into the dark siding where the rails are headed, but there's no tube train coming. It's the ringing of a year ago, the wheezing and puffing that went on day and night as I lay in that other tunnel.

Step by step, I go into the gloom until I'm past the danger of the rails.

Gigantic iron girders run upwards along the tunnel's walls; their job is to ensure it doesn't collapse. Between each girder there's space for one blanket; a narrow bed for a man, a woman or a child.

I look at each sleeping body in the half-light, each turned-away cheek, each hand, each arm.

But when I finally get there, I recognise him instantly.

There's Jack.

He's taken off his shirt; it hangs on a spike above his head. His vest looks white in the semi-darkness but it's probably just as filthy as the rest of his clothes. He's lying on his side with his cheek resting on his arm; his eyes are closed.

Right next to him, in the last spot before the tunnel ends, there's Quinn. She didn't go to her fancy hotel, she isn't roaming the streets in desperation, she's here. Lying down next to Jack.

I stand and look at them in silence. How peacefully they're sleeping. It's as though they belong together. I press my nails into the palm of my hand, but I can't stop staring.

Then I see the notebook with all my stories in Jack's hand.

9

If I hesitate now, I'll never do it.

Quinn's lying right next to Jack, but there's still some room on the other side of him. A space between two girders where nobody's sleeping. I get on my knees and crawl as quietly as I can towards him.

Without looking at his face, I take hold of the corner of my notebook. So slowly I hardly move, I pull it from his sleeping hand. But the moment I have it, I feel his fingers around my wrist.

I recoil. "Ouch!"

He sits up and rubs his eyes with one hand. His other hand has my wrist in an iron grip.

"Let go of me," I whisper. "Jack, that hurts!"

"Ella?" he asks in surprise.

I hear my breathing quicken. I'm doing it wrong, exactly the way the doctors said I shouldn't breathe.

"This is mine," I say.

Jack looks at the notebook in my hand and I see he only remembers about it now. His teeth shine in the darkness. He is grinning.

"Oh yeah. How funny. Ella's diary."

His grasp loosens and I pull myself free. I scramble to my feet and begin to limp as fast as I can back out of the tunnel. My head is pounding. I know I can never outpace Jack, but if I can get to the platform, I have a chance. It's brightly lit there, people are awake and I can ask for help.

But Jack doesn't come after me.

What did I think? That he wanted to clutch my stories to his chest for the rest of his life?

I look back over my shoulder again but it's all quiet.

I climb back on to the platform with difficulty. There's a stabbing pain in my leg. I walk as fast as I can past the slop bucket and folding screen. There are people lying all over the floor. The fug of sweat and the rumbling chorus of snores float above the platform, and suddenly I find myself unable to go on.

I'm suffocating.

Of all the people who could have found my stories, it had to be Jack.

And then I hear footsteps.

He comes strolling casually out of the tunnel, jumps smoothly up on to the platform and disappears behind the screen.

I still can't move. The air is heavy on my shoulders. In a flash I wonder how many feet we are below the ground. Everyone is sheltering here because it feels safe, far from the bombs. But what if one fell on the station? What if the booking hall collapsed and there was no way out? We'd be trapped.

"Ella?"

I turn round. There he is. He's rebuttoned his trousers.

With a shaking hand, I wipe my hair out of my face. It feels greasy. I can't remember the last time I washed it.

I don't want to say anything to him, but I can't help it.

"Did Quinn read it too?" I whisper. I hold up my book; he shakes his head.

We're on the draughtiest part of the platform, close to the escalators. Most people avoid lying here.

"You can't tell her anything," I insist. "It's not a diary. It's nonsense. I made it all up."

"Oh really?" he asks calmly.

"Of course!" I almost start crying. "Do you think they really brought me flowers and baskets of fruit? That my whole class came to sing under my window? That anywhere in the world there's a doctor who would kiss a polio patient?"

He begins to chuckle softly. "Is that what you wrote?"

A cold wind blows through my hair from the passageway. I feel the blood drain from my face.

"You haven't read it?"

"Nah. Your handwriting's awful. And I left school ages ago. I've forgotten at least half the letters." He starts to laugh, more loudly now. "Blimey, I had no idea it was actually worth reading!"

A woman on the floor whispers for us to quieten down and a man gives us a threatening look.

I don't say anything else.

I know I have to sleep but I can't go back to my bed. My blood is racing too fast, the air is too thick, I'll go mad if I have to lie on the floor again.

On the wall next to me there's an arrow with six letters above it. WAY OUT.

Without giving Jack another glance, I leave the platform.

10

I don't know where I'm going, only that I need to get away. I walk through the shiny, echoing passageways, past rows of bodies rolled up in blankets. A little girl lies close to the wall to make space for her doll in a neatly made-up bed.

And then I stop.

The towering escalators have been paused, and I can hardly believe it – people are sleeping here too. They are draped over the steps, half sitting, half lying. Heads rest on a bag or a folded sweater. Men in suits, young women who have to go to work as usual in the morning.

There's no blood, no sirens, no gunshots. There isn't a soldier to be seen, no Churchill, no Hitler. Nothing but ordinary people. My eyes fill with tears.

One of the three escalators has been left free for people who are mad enough to want to go up or down in the middle of the night.

I carefully put my right foot on the first step, then haul up my left leg. A two-year-old climbs stairs like this. This is how I will do it for the rest of my life. After twenty steps, I stop to catch my breath, again after forty and then sixty.

By the time I've reached the top, my legs are burning. Even in the booking hall, there are people sleeping. I listen out for sirens, whether there are bombs falling above ground, but it's quiet. I hurry on, up the last short flight of steps and then I'm outside on a windy pavement in an inky street.

The cold air still smells of smoke. There's no moon; the city is plunged in darkness. A strip of light shining through curtains is forbidden; the street lamps are out; you're not even allowed to smoke a cigarette outside. Boy scouts have painted the edges of the pavements white, and pedestrians have to carry a white hanky or wear a white scarf so they don't get run over in the darkness of the blackout.

The entire city anxiously obeys the rules, but the bombers don't give a damn. They follow the glittering water of the Thames from the coast to London before cheerfully dumping a load of incendiary bombs on the city. Then the next wave of planes can see exactly where they need to be.

I feel goosebumps on my arms but don't even think about going back inside. Everything that has happened today is whirling about my head. And then I think: *If Quinn can, I can.*

I can choose.

I'll have a limp for the rest of my life, I know that.

But I don't have to spend the rest of my life being afraid.

It's at that moment I hear the air-raid warning. One siren starts to wail and then dozens of other sirens join in. It's a terrifying sound that swells repeatedly, and everyone in

London knows they've got twelve minutes. By then the first planes will have reached the city and all hell will break loose again.

The houses hold their breath. The anti-aircraft guns are brought into position. Searchlights will soon sweep the skies.

And I stand there in the darkness and open the notebook. I pull out the first pages and tear them into a hundred pieces. I open my hands, and the fragments are carried away by the wind.

As fast as I can, I tear out the next pages. I have at least nine minutes left. More fragments are blown from my palms. All those silly make-believes, all those castles in the air, simply vanish into the night.

I carry on until I reach the last page.

And then I hear the roar of engines. I stand very still on the dark pavement.

I can choose.

I think of that night at home when I hid under the stairs with Robbie. I wasn't scared when I heard the bomb whistling.

And I think of the tunnels deep below my feet, tunnels full of bodies you can hear and see and smell and feel. I realise I've forgotten how to be around more than a handful of people.

And then I choose.

Before the first planes have dropped their bombs, I've turned round and gone back inside.

11

How do you start again?

I wake up and don't feel any less afraid than the day before. Every muscle in my body is stiff. I haven't done my leg exercises all week.

The platform guard cries in a loud voice, "All clear! Leave the platform and please vacate the station!"

And here we go again. Blankets piled into the cart, the metal box with our ID cards, the coupon books and all our money at the bottom. The whole world needs a bath but a week ago the public baths were turned into mortuaries. There isn't enough space to keep all the bodies otherwise.

"There you are, Ella!"

I stop and look up.

Quinn cuts through the slow-moving crowd with her enormous case. The air lightens immediately: she hasn't forgotten me. Her blouse is crumpled; there's a perfect streak of dirt on her cheek. This is what a film star looks like after her first night of war.

"Thank god you're up and about again!" She walks alongside me. "I let you down dreadfully yesterday. I'm sorry… But what was the matter? Are you ill?"

"I hadn't eaten enough."

"That's incredibly foolish of you," she says, relieved. "Now I know why you're so thin."

We trail behind my family through the crowded white passageways and every three steps another man offers to carry her case. Each time, she shakes her head determinedly.

"It's a trap," she says to me. "You only have to say, 'Oh yes, please – do carry my case a while,' and they immediately respond with, 'Weakling! No more work for you! You can spend your life bearing children!'"

I don't reply. In all the months I've shuffled around London with a limp, not one man has ever offered to help me. They don't want to have children with me, so they don't bother to carry my suitcase.

Quinn steps on to the up escalator out of breath. Her cheeks are glowing; she looks ready for any fight.

"I'm going to look for a job today! Imagine, I might get a job in a shop. Or as a waitress, with a nice apron…"

"Will you stay in that fancy hotel then?"

"Are you mad? I'm coming back here tonight. I sleep so well lying next to Jack. Even his sweat smells nice!"

I ball my fists but say nothing. She doesn't have to know that I was in the tunnel last night, how long I stared at her and Jack as they lay so close to each other.

We climb the last flight of steps to street level. Grey pigeons flap across a sky without bombers; a fire engine drives past. And then Quinn stops.

She stands there, frozen.

People flow around her through the exit, but she doesn't notice. She's staring across the street at the pavement packed with dusty backs hurriedly disappearing into the morning light.

"Sebastian!" she shouts as hard as she can. Her voice cracks. "Seb! Wait for me!"

The rest of the world has stopped existing. She lets go of her case and without a word to me she begins to run. She crosses the street, joins the dozens of people on the pavement, and then she's gone.

I stand there with her deadweight of a case.

My family are still walking ahead, but Robbie runs back in concern. He stops right in front of me.

"Why aren't you coming?" He looks at my face as though I'm the younger child and he's already grown up. "Are you going to faint again?"

I shake my head. "I need to watch Quinn's case. Tell Mum I'll be along in a bit."

I've no idea whether Quinn's coming back. Maybe I'm mad to wait for her.

"Ella…" Robbie takes a run-up and scales a pillar box, an enormous red one, and sits there. "We can go to the zoo on my birthday, can't we? There won't still be bombs then, will there?"

"Of course we'll go," I say immediately. "We go every year, don't we? If we have to, we'll go between the air raids."

"Promise?" He looks down at me from the blood-red post box with a serious expression. "Even if Dad's too tired and Mum's with all those homeless people, you'll take me?"

"Promise," I reply. Two and a half weeks is an eternity when there are bombs falling every night.

Robbie stands up, spreads his arms and jumps down without hesitating. I hold my breath, but he lands on his feet and begins to run again.

"I'll tell Mum you'll come along soon," he shouts back. "And I want to see the monkeys first at the zoo!"

I look at him and shiver. My happy, skinny brother who is never tired and never ill. He disappears round the corner, leaving me all alone.

I slowly button up my woolly cardigan. The street is covered in shrapnel from the anti-aircraft guns. On this same spot I tore out page after page of my notebook. The strips of paper have gone. My made-up life has gone.

I have nothing left but this. My real life.

And then I see Quinn approaching. She's walking slowly. The bounce has gone from her step; the pavement is made of stone again. She doesn't look up until she's beside me.

"I thought I never wanted to see him again." Her chin quivers. "I thought I didn't miss him."

I want to say something, but she stamps her foot. "I don't *want* to miss him. He isn't worth it. It's a miracle they haven't thrown him into jail, because that's where he belongs."

"Who?" I ask. "Sebastian?"

She shakes her head. "We don't talk about him any more. We don't mention his name."

"But you just shouted out his name! And now you're talking about him, aren't you? Who's Sebastian?"

She's pale. "He was my brother."

A cart drives past, loaded with furniture covered in plaster dust. The sound of the horse's hooves echoes through the street.

"Is he dead?" I ask gently.

"To us he is. We haven't seen him for more than a year."

"But he was just here!" I cry. "Did you talk to him?"

She shakes her head. "I ran across half the city but when I finally caught up with him, it was somebody else…" She picks up her suitcase decisively. "He doesn't exist any more. Believe me, it's for the best."

"You're mad. How can that be good?"

She presses her lips together into a stiff smile. "Goodbye, Ella. Thank you for looking after my case. I'm going to drop my luggage off with Old William and then look for a job."

I watch her walk away in her much too baggy trousers and I'm about to lower my eyes and go home. But then I think about the previous night. The excitement I felt when I thought about not having to spend the rest of my life waiting for the whistle of the next bomb. The fact I have a choice.

"Quinn!" I call out. "Wait for me!"

She turns round.

She's crying. Not like a film star but like my five-year-old neighbour. Her face is drawn. Tears run down her cheeks; snot shines on her top lip.

"Come with me," I say. "You can leave your case at our house. There aren't any lice there, and my mother will have a pan of porridge ready. After that, you can look for a job."

She stands and gazes at me in silence. She raises her chin but says nothing.

I begin to walk towards her.

When I'm almost at her side, she suddenly shakes her head. "I can't act like Sebastian doesn't exist! I have to see him. Will you come with me? I can't face him alone."

12

Quinn is taller than me, she can run a hundred times faster, she's got a dizzying amount of money. And yet she's asking me to help her. I thought she was fearless.

"Is your brother dangerous?" I feel the goosebumps on my arms. "Are you frightened of him?"

"No," she says at once. "I'm frightened of myself. I don't know what I'll do if I see him again, what I'll say to him."

I think of all the fancy words dancing around Quinn's mind and wonder how many swear words she came across in that dictionary of hers.

"All right," I say. "I'll come with you." I straighten my shoulders. For a whole year my life only took place on paper. Now I want more. "But on one condition. I need to know what he did."

"Deal," she says earnestly. "But first, it's time for porridge! Which way is it?"

"Really? You want to come and eat porridge at ours?"

"Yes, please."

She begins to walk and before I've even begun to catch my breath again, she's in our kitchen.

Perhaps this wasn't such a good idea.

Our kitchen is half under street level. Its small windows are steamed up; it always smells musty. My mother is stirring a big pan of oatmeal porridge, and I suddenly notice how grey she is. I look at our narrow table with its worn tablecloth, the teapot's leaky spout, the vests and stockings hanging to dry on a rack in the corner.

"I'd like to freshen up," Quinn says to me quietly.

"There's the tap." I point at the sink.

"In the bathroom, I mean."

"We don't have a bathroom. We wash ourselves in the kitchen."

"But…" She whispers now. "I need to pee."

"Oh, of course." I lead her up the creaking staircase, open the back door and point out the tiny toilet in the courtyard. "We share it with the people upstairs. The right-hand side is the coal shed, the left the toilet. There should still be a few bits of newspaper on the hook."

"To read?" she asks in amazement.

I hear Robbie chuckling behind me. "To wipe your backside, of course!" he says.

I begin to giggle, but Quinn looks worried.

"Ella, I didn't realise how poor your family was. Do you have enough porridge for me?"

"We're not poor," I say. "We have three rooms, there are no rats, we all have shoes, and Dad has a steady job. Now hurry up. We're about to eat."

*

"Tell me then!" We're walking along the street together and I'm the girl from the previous afternoon again. I feel new. "What did your brother do? Do you know where to find him? What's our plan?"

Mum went to the Women's Voluntary Service straight after breakfast. She thinks I'm spending the morning at home. At two o'clock I have to relieve my aunt in the queue for the Underground – this time, no messing about. But we can do whatever we want until then.

For example, we might just go in search of the outcast son whose name can no longer be mentioned.

Quinn is wearing a green dress with puff sleeves and a white belt. I stood there open-mouthed when she tipped her handbag out over her case in my bedroom earlier. Gold bracelets fell jingling on to her clothes, earrings with matt-gloss pearls, a chain with a sapphire pendant, a dazzling diamond tiara.

"Is that all yours?" I'd whispered.

"Pretty much."

"*Pretty much?*"

"Well, I'm the youngest. So everything that belongs to my mother and sisters will be mine one day."

I had plenty of questions about this but I held my tongue. Then Quinn threw a gold ring and two earrings with tiny rubies into her handbag, closed her suitcase and slid it under my bed.

I'd frowned. "Is that really the best hiding place?"

"The ideal one, I think. Nobody's going to come and search your three rooms without rats, are they? Or do you think my jewellery is safer with Jack?"

And now we're walking through London together, through streets I've known all my life but that suddenly feel exciting. The sun is shining brightly; summer has only just ended.

"Tell me then," I repeat. "You can't expect me to help you face Sebastian without having a clue what's going on."

Quinn sighs. "I expect you've let your imagination run away with you. You're picturing a mystery with a young lord and a country manor, something incredibly romantic. Admit it! What do you think he's done?"

"Gambled away all your money, got a girl pregnant or murdered someone," I reply immediately.

She bursts out laughing. "Golly! You should write a novel!"

"I want to." I've said it out loud now.

"Really? You want to be a writer?"

I nod. "Of course I won't manage it. But I do want to."

Quinn puts two fingers in her mouth and before I know it, a taxi has stopped for us.

"Why wouldn't you manage it?" she asks as we get in. "You don't need a tennis court or diamonds for that. A pen and paper, that's enough. And ideas. Well, you have enough of those." She looks at the cabbie. "Would you be so kind as to take us to the Royal Albert Hall. Thank you."

With a hard tug, she closes the window between the driver and the back seat and then turns to me. "How much do you know about politics?"

"Um, well… I know there's a war on."

I hear how stupid this sounds but I can still hardly believe it: I told her I wanted to be a writer and she didn't laugh at me.

"You must know who Sir Oswald Mosley is?" Quinn says as we head westwards. Away from the poverty-stricken slums towards London's rich, elegant side.

"He's in politics then?" And then I sigh. "I really have no idea. I was ill for a year. Before that I was in a secret club called Girls Who Climb Trees, and Robbie and I tried to teach the baker's dog tricks. That was about it."

"That sounds wonderful," Quinn says before becoming serious. "So Oswald Mosley was sent to prison four months ago for being a fascist. A real one. Hitler was guest of honour at his wedding a few years back. That says enough if you ask me."

"Is he German?"

She shakes her head. "English. He's the leader of the British Union of Fascists. A filthy traitor. He thought we should just let Hitler get on with it in Europe. Hitler could occupy Poland, the Netherlands, Belgium and France, just as long as he left Great Britain alone."

I want to listen, but London is bustling outside the taxi window. Buildings flash by – grey, white and a dull reddish colour – with lots of stone ornaments and fairy-tale turrets.

There are gigantic advertisements on the walls for raincoats and Jacob's Cream Crackers; there's a long queue in front of a butcher's. And then there's a sudden gap in the row of houses. The walls end with ragged burned edges, the street is still wet from the water used to put out the fire.

"Did you hear what I said?" Quinn asks impatiently. "That monster Mosley wanted to do a deal with Hitler. If we left Hitler alone, he'd leave us alone. Not because Mosley was such a pacifist, oh no. He had his own band of thugs to fight for him."

"A band of thugs?" I ask. "Here in England?"

"Yes, the Blackshirts. His own private army of uniformed bullies. Mosley didn't really believe in democracy. If people didn't want to listen, they'd have to be forced. He had the Blackshirts beat up all his opponents. Jews and communists and everyone who didn't agree with him. But Sebastian..."

She stops.

I finally take my eyes off the streets outside. I see her face and my heart begins to race.

"Sebastian agreed with him, you see," says Quinn.

"With Mosley?" I ask. "With Hitler's chum?" I can hardly believe it. "Your brother's a fascist?"

She nods.

"And we're on our way to see him?"

"Yes, he's at university here and he lives round the corner from the Royal Albert Hall. I don't suppose you've happened to see a concert there by any chance?"

"We happen to spend all our money on three rooms without rats," I say.

We drive on in silence.

I daren't look at Quinn. I thought she had everything. Shiny lips and diamonds and not giving a damn about the rest of the world. When you walk along beside her, the air sparkles.

But she's got a brother who is a traitor.

I try to imagine Robbie doing something despicable. Something that would make me never want to see him again. Something that would make me loathe the ground he walked on.

I imagine this and feel an abyss as deep as the train tunnels under the city.

Does Quinn feel this dizzy when she thinks about her brother? I can't ask. The taxi is driving too fast – we're almost there. The streets become wider, the buildings grander, and then we drive along Hyde Park.

"That grass looks dreadful!" Quinn says, shocked. "So much mud! Aren't the parks looked after here?"

"They dug trenches in the grass," I say curtly. "They put metal covers over them and now they're shelters."

"Seriously?" she asks. "Do people really shelter in those trenches? Every night? The whole night long?"

I nod.

"My god!" Quinn exclaims. "I really feel like beating Sebastian up."

13

Sebastian doesn't look a bit like a Nazi.

He's wearing green pyjamas and a bright red dressing gown. His hair is combed, he's holding a cigarette, and his smile is positively heartwarming.

He opens the door wide so that we can see his whole room. There are two ancient leather armchairs, a folding screen with a cherry-blossom pattern, and on a table next to the open window, a gramophone is playing. The music is hypnotic – a jazzy trumpet leads the way, the other instruments follow.

We've found him.

The taxi took us to the Royal Albert Hall, and once we'd walked around the enormous, cake-shaped concert hall, Quinn knew where to go.

"The students live round the corner there!" she cried. "We went to see them once last year in the summertime. Before Sebastian came to study here. When I could still call him my brother…"

The porter almost wouldn't let us in, but Quinn was able to show her identity card and prove she was an actual family member, not some girl trying to get herself knocked up by a lord.

It didn't matter who I was. I walked into a different world with my old gingham dress and my gammy leg. An impressive red-brick building rose up around a square courtyard, and for the first time in my life I saw real students.

They were wearing expensive suits and striped ties and shiny, polished shoes. A laughing group sat in deckchairs on the grass and there was music coming from an open window that made me want to dance.

That was his music, the fascist's.

And now here we are, face to face.

"Quinn!" Sebastian cries. "Quinny, you've come!"

He beams, dimples appearing in his cheeks, and opens his arms wide.

But Quinn doesn't throw herself into his waiting hug. She stands next to me on the doorstep, her eyes almost black.

She takes a deep breath and steps past Sebastian into the room. Without saying a word, she pulls the window shut and takes the needle off the gramophone record.

She looks her brother in the eye in the deathly silent room.

"I hope you feel it," she says quietly. She balls her fists. "I hope you feel every bomb that falls. Every house that collapses, every child that gets burned or buried under the rubble…"

"What?" The dimples disappear from his cheeks.

"God knows, I feel it." There are tears in her eyes. "I'm jealous of people who can simply curse Hitler without being reminded each time that their very own brother is a fascist too."

"Enough," says Sebastian.

But Quinn is unstoppable.

"I thought I knew you! You were the only one in our stupid family who got me. It was the two of us against the rest, until you suddenly turned into a Nazi!"

Sebastian puts his cigarette out, irritated. "Will you let me speak?"

"No," she shouts. "I won't believe you if you say Mosley's not a fascist. Even the government agrees with me, that's why they've thrown that traitor in prison. I just don't understand why you're still allowed to study here. I wouldn't want a dirty turncoat like you in my class!"

Sebastian gets to Quinn in two steps. He puts his hands on her shoulders, and she immediately begins to thump him. Without speaking he grabs her wrists.

"Let her go!" I cry.

I'm standing next to the door with my back to the wall. They completely ignore me.

"Listen." Sebastian is barely taller than his sister, and slender. But he's stronger than her. "I was impressed by Mosley, I'll admit that. The man is a brilliant speaker. So yes, I was intrigued. But you were the ones who went crazy when I wanted to go to his rally."

"You think that's odd?" Quinn rages. "The biggest fascist rally ever to be held in England. And you wanted to attend it?!"

"You acted crazy," he repeats. "Not just Mama and Papa but Gussie and Vi and Cee and you. You acted like I was the devil. As though everything I'd done and thought for nineteen years had simply been erased. So I went." He sighs. "And that was the first and last time I saw Mosley. He has a silver tongue but the man's a cad. And a fascist. And I'm not."

He lets go of her wrists, straightens his dressing gown and lights a new cigarette.

I wait for the moment that Quinn begins to laugh in relief. But it doesn't come.

She frowns. "You haven't had anything to do with Mosley for over a year?" Her voice is soft. "And you're prepared to fight against the Nazis now?"

"Absolutely."

"And all that time you didn't think it was necessary to tell us? We thought you were a traitor! I thought you were a traitor. If only you'd written me a letter. If only you'd explained – at least to me…"

He blows out a big puff of smoke and runs a hand over his hair. And then he sighs. "I don't need to tell you what things are like at home. I had to get away, sever ties."

"And me, then?"

"You were an unfortunate casualty."

She takes a step back, and I think of the ports that are bombed each night. Hitler wants to flatten them to stop supplies reaching London. The fact that thousands of workers live next to the ports in tiny houses with their families – well, that's just bad luck. Unfortunate casualties. Every war has its unintended victims.

It works the same in families, apparently.

"I know that our parents aren't monsters," Sebastian says. "They're blocks of stone. Rocks that have existed since the beginning of the world. If you kick them, nothing changes. You just break your toes. What happened last year made me finally understand. They only love you if you're exactly like them."

"So you saved your own skin," Quinn says. "And you left me behind."

He doesn't reply. His face is drawn.

I think of the swinging trumpet leading the band, and I wish I could hear the music again. But I realise we're done here.

"Oh well," Quinn says in her perfect radio voice. "So I was right all along. You're a scumbag." She straightens her shoulders. "And a traitor." She sticks her nose in the air. "And a coward."

She walks to the door, her chin raised high. "Come on, Ella, we're leaving."

Sebastian looks at me for the first time. His eyes are just as dark as Quinn's, his face is pale. I can tell that he's breaking inside, but he's too well brought up to let it show.

I give a kind of awkward wave. "Hello. I'm Ella. Erm – bye then."

14

We cut right across the sunny courtyard, each step taking us further away from Sebastian. I don't belong here, that's clear. Mine's a family of Cockneys; for centuries we've hardly been to school; for centuries we've been too poor to sit and laugh in a deckchair all day. And yet I'm sure I'm coming back here.

I have to see Sebastian again.

Quinn walks beside me, as straight as a pole. There's no doubt about it – she's a member of the rock family at this moment. Inside my head I hear her saying, *You were the only one in our stupid family who got me. It was the two of us against the rest.* And I shudder.

Two days ago, I was standing in the queue for the Underground. Jack looked at me and for a second I thought he could see it. Who I am if you forget my leg and my mousy hair. For a moment I thought he understood me. And during that one moment, the world felt a little lighter.

So Quinn actually has that, someone who understands her. And yet she screams at him as the city collapses and nobody knows who'll still be alive tomorrow.

I don't say anything, but I've made up my mind: those two need to make up.

Just before we leave the courtyard garden, I hear music again. This time a crystal-clear female voice comes out of the window. Her words float above the laughing students, and I recognise the song, it's "Over the Rainbow".

I keep listening to the melody as we walk away until the tooting of double-decker buses, the ringing bells of fire engines and the cries of newspaper vendors drown out the last notes.

Quinn remains silent all the way back home. I would love to ask her what Sebastian meant when he said, "I don't need to tell you what things are like at home", but I daren't. What's so terrible there at that country house whose name she doesn't want to tell me? What could be so awful it made Sebastian feel he had to escape the place a year ago and Quinn run away this week? Is it so unbearable having horses and a tennis court and a butler?

Just before the taxi draws up at my house, Quinn says, "Why don't you take a nap for an hour. I have to run a couple of errands."

"I don't want a nap! I'm not tired at all."

"You're exhausted," she says calmly. "You didn't sleep a wink last night, did you?"

She looks at me and her face is no longer made of stone. I almost burst out crying.

"That platform drives me crazy. Really. Completely crazy."

"Why?"

I hesitate. She doesn't know anything about my illness; all she's seen is my leg.

"I had to go into quarantine last year – for a long time. There was no other way. I did get better but now there's something wrong with my brain."

"Is there?"

I nod. "Normal people seem dangerous. Even when they don't do anything bad. They breathe, that's enough. And they do that the whole time on the platform. And the light keeps on flickering and there are people snogging and old people peeing and the trains coming and going…"

"And above ground, bombs are falling," says Quinn. "And that might not make you crazy, but it would make you flat."

I wait for her to laugh but she keeps a straight face. She opens her handbag and holds up the earrings. The rubies sparkle like fresh drops of blood.

"I'm going to sell these and then I'll have enough money to last a while. I'll buy a place for you in the tunnel tonight. It's dark and quiet and nobody walks past. You'll sleep well there."

I stare at her. "You want me to sleep in the tunnel tonight?"

She nods.

"With you and Jack? And you'll pay him money for it?"

"Certainly. If a charming lad is prepared to save a couple of places for us, I'm happy to make use of that."

*

I'm breathless for the rest of the day. I know Quinn can't force me to sleep in the tunnel. I also know that my mother will never agree to it.

But as I lie in bed, trying to nap before I have to take my aunt's place in the queue, there are a few seconds when I think I'll do it. I want to lie next to Quinn and Jack in the dark, hundreds of feet from my family. Away from the light, away from the noisy rows of sardines. I want to lie in a tunnel that smells of Jack's sweat.

But then I think of that other tunnel again. I remember the panic that came over me when I woke up and my body was no longer my own. A machine was in control. My head stuck out, but my body was completely out of reach.

The tunnel didn't only wreck my brain but the rest of me too. Before those weeks in hospital, my body had just been a tool. I could run with it, and climb, and skip with a rope and kick tin cans. I never thought about the different parts.

And now I do. I lie in bed and slowly run my fingers over my skin. The skin of my arms, my thighs, my belly… It started when I came home from hospital, when I had to keep checking if my body still worked, whether I could still move and hadn't lost sensation anywhere.

And now, even though I don't have to check any more, I keep doing it. I run my fingers over my skin, and I know I have to stop but I can't.

*

I didn't think it would happen in a thousand years, but Quinn manages it: my mother agrees. Without me even adding a word to the conversation, they decide that I'm going to sleep in the tunnel. They talk about me like I'm still a patient. A vegetable that's going to wither on a brightly lit, packed, noisy platform.

I don't stop them. I let it happen while feeling my breathing become shallower and shallower.

First, we have dinner with my family. It's a special meal because Quinn has been shopping. There are prunes and Garibaldi biscuits, and she gets a tin of corned beef for sandwiches out of her handbag.

And then it's time to go to the tunnel. Quinn has bought a dark blue blanket. I get my flowery bedspread. Robbie is furious he's not allowed to come with us, but our mother stands her ground. He has to sleep next to her.

"Does Jack know I'm coming?" I whisper as we weave our way through the sea of people.

Quinn shakes her head. "I haven't seen him since this morning. I reserved two places for myself – I didn't feel like having a stranger next to me. So you can lie there."

The packed platform now looks like a shabby sitting room. People have brought all kinds of stuff with them for the night: folding stools and teapots and slippers and chessboards. A man keeps playing "London Bridge Is Falling Down" on the harmonica, three babies are competing to see who can cry the loudest and the warm musty air smells of beer.

We get closer to the tunnel, and I don't know what I'm more scared of: the gaping black hole or seeing Jack.

I briefly hope he'll be a disappointment now. This morning I saw Sebastian, the first lord I've seen in my life. A lord with a heartwarming smile and a room filled with cherry blossom and music.

But Jack is no disappointment. The only disappointment is me. I see it in his gaze. He was expecting Quinn. On her own.

"What's she doing here?" he asks immediately. He points at me without looking at me.

"Sheltering," Quinn says cheerfully. "Unfortunately, they're dropping quite a few bombs above ground." She puts down her blanket and sits next to him. "I'm paying for both of us… This one's left over if—"

She holds up the corned beef sandwich she'd kept especially for him, and he almost rips it out of her hands. As I stand there motionlessly, he eats with big, greedy bites, wolfing the food like a starving stray dog.

"If I were you," says Quinn, "I'd take a look at my business model. How can you be so hungry if you earn money each day? Where's all the money going?"

"None of your business." He stuffs the last crust in his mouth and licks his fingers.

I want to say something but can't. The back of my head is tingling; needles stab into my neck.

"Ella?" Quinn says. "Do you want…"

The tunnel blurs; I stagger.

"Look out!" she cries.

Before I can fall, Jack is at my side. I feel his arm around my waist. The dark walls are spinning and we sink to the ground together, but it doesn't hurt because he's holding me.

"Head between your knees," he says gruffly.

I obey and feel the blood flow back to my head, his arm still around my waist.

I sit in silence.

He wolfs his food like a stray dog, I tell myself.

His clothes are dirty. You can see from all his muscles that he spends the whole day lugging heavy things around and drudging away.

He's forgotten half the letters of the alphabet.

But maybe, if I sit very, very still, he will do the same.

15

"This isn't a good idea, Ella." Quinn's voice reaches me from a distance. "If you're ill, you must sleep with your family."

I look up and Jack immediately gets to his feet. Without saying anything, he sits back down next to Quinn.

"I'm not ill."

"Yes, you are." She lowers her voice. "We might have to call a doctor and then the police will come too, of course. And then I'll have to hotfoot it."

"Me too," Jack says. "Well, then it's obvious. Ella will have to leave." He gives Quinn an interested look. "Are you on the run?"

She sighs. "Maybe. It depends whether they want me back at home or not. And if my mother suddenly decides to polish her tiara, that would also do it..."

"I'm not sick," I cry. "I'm scared!"

They stare at me in the half-light. They're shocked. Everyone's scared but nobody says it. You stay calm, you clench your teeth and you carry on. Day after day. Until Hitler has been beaten.

But I can't hold my tongue any more. I have to tell them this.

"I got ill a year ago." My voice quivers but I carry on. "It began with a stabbing headache, and then a fever. And when I woke up the next morning, my leg had gone lame."

"Polio," Quinn says at once.

We all know the list of diseases you never want to catch. Tuberculosis. Diphtheria. Measles. Pneumonia. Polio.

We all know families with holes in them. Siblings that have lost a little brother or sister. Babies that never made it past their first birthday.

"Yes," I say. "Polio. They took me to hospital and the paralysis got worse. When I stopped being able to breathe, they put me in an iron lung."

I hear a thud in the distance. The ground shakes under my palms.

"An iron lung?" Jack asks. "What the hell's that?"

"A machine." I swallow. "A tunnel that breathes for you."

Quinn and Jack are the only people who can hear me.

Side by side, they sit against the wall with me opposite them. The tunnel is blocked to my left. Months ago, they stopped digging there: it's dark and quiet. In a long row to my right, people are sleeping between the rock-hard girders, but they aren't listening to our conversation. The three of us have this little patch of the underground world to ourselves.

"An iron lung is a tube on legs," I say quietly, "as long as a man. You're slid into it on a stretcher and then it closes. Your body lies inside it, only your head sticks out. There's a bit of rubber round your neck because it has to be airtight."

I don't dare look at Jack, I only look at Quinn. But I know he's listening too.

"A giant pair of bellows pumps air around your body, squeezing the air out of your lungs. Then the bellows suck all the air back out and your lungs fill up again. That way you can breathe without breathing,"

"Does it feel odd?" Quinn asks.

"It's creepy. Like your body's not yours any more."

In my mind, I hear the constant whoosh of the bellows again. It was deafening, but I was also terrified it would stop. If there was a power cut, I'd suffocate in the tunnel.

"How did you cope?" Quinn whispers.

"I didn't. Can't you tell? I keep fainting whenever I think about it…" I clear my throat. "You lie there waiting to get better, flat on your back. Some people die in the tunnel. Others can never breathe on their own again and have to stay in the iron lung."

"My god. Their whole lives?"

"Nobody knows. The machines haven't been around that long. No one has had time to get old in an iron lung yet."

All this time, I've avoided looking at Jack's face. I can only see the black toes of his big, scuffed workman's shoes. I hear him breathing a little too quickly.

And I carry on talking because I want him to know what it was like.

I don't want that idiot ever to turn his leg in and pretend to have a limp again.

"Were your parents there?" Quinn asks. "In the hospital?"

"No. I could have infected them, so they had to go into quarantine along with Robbie. They weren't allowed out of the house for two weeks. My aunt left a bag of food in front of the door each day. And I…"

I stop.

"I lay there, and I was scared of dying without ever seeing them again."

Jack makes a sudden movement. "Well, now we know!" He sniffs noisily. "It all turned out all right, didn't it? You can breathe again, you can hobble along. It's just when you see a tunnel, you pass out."

Quinn gives him a shove. "Hush! Ella's telling us a horrific story. You could be a—"

"You think this is horrific?" he interrupts. "Really?" He sounds furious. "She had polio. She got the best new treatment. God knows who paid for it, probably some charity or other that belongs to rich idiots. And she survived. I wish all the suffering in the world was that simple."

I sit there as quiet as a mouse. I wrap my fingers around the iron girder next to me.

"You're a rotten swine," Quinn says. "Men are such cads—"

She stops because someone is walking towards us. I see a pair of skinny knees covered in scabs, sleeves that are already too short.

"It's not fair at all!" Robbie stops and puts his hands on his hips. "Why do I have to sleep on the platform with those boring grown-ups? All they do is talk about the milkman's baby and complain about the baker's wife's big feet. I want to sleep next to you."

It feels like we've been living under the ground for weeks. Like I've suddenly woken up.

I clear my throat. "Does Mother know you're here?"

"Of course not! I scarpered." He lifts his chin. "There's a war on. I want to live."

I sigh and make to stand up, but Quinn is quicker than me.

"Don't get up, Ella! I'll do it." She lays her hand on Robbie's shoulder. "Come along, soldier." She looks at me. "Stay conscious, please." And then in a strict tone to Jack: "I haven't finished what I was saying about men being scoundrels. Don't think you can get away with it that easily. I'll talk to you later."

She turns round and guides Robbie back to the brightly lit platform.

Jack and I stay behind alone.

16

We sit facing each other in the tunnel, not speaking.

I stare at the ground and inside my head I can hear his words: *It all turned out all right, didn't it? You can breathe again, you can hobble along.*

Yes, I can breathe again.

I had to learn how to.

Before I was allowed out of the tunnel for a couple of minutes that first time, the doctors had to explain to me how to breathe. They told me exactly which muscles to use, that my belly had to come forward and my shoulders had to stay low.

And then they opened the hatch and pulled me out.

It was scarier than almost dying in the iron lung. Suddenly, it was up to me to make sure I stayed alive.

Imagine learning to fly. You wouldn't make your first flight in the middle of the night during an air raid. You'd pick a summer's day without any wind. But you don't get to choose a safe way to practise breathing. There's no shallow water, no summer's day without Messerschmitts.

If you do it wrong, you die.

It was scarier than sitting here in the dark tunnel with Jack.

I raise my eyes and look him straight in the face. "So if polio's not scary to you, what is?"

He looks back at me. I see the angular line of his jaw, his dark eyebrows.

He shrugs indifferently. "What does it matter? Every family on my street has some gruesome story. But we don't bother each other with them."

"I don't believe you."

"Oh no?"

"No! People love misery. Particularly other people's misery. That's why they read books, that's why they buy newspapers, that's why they gossip with their neighbours." I fold my arms. "So what's your story?"

I look at him and see it happen. The indifference disappears from his face for a second.

"You want to hear my story?" he asks. "Really?"

"Yes," I say.

For at least half a minute I think he's going to remain silent.

But then he begins to speak. His voice is flat, his eyes fixed on the inky walls of the tunnel.

"My dad," he says, "he never keeps the same job for more than three days. He was in the trenches in Flanders in the last war and my ma always said his body survived that war but his soul didn't." He shrugs. "That's nonsense, of course, but the truth is, there ain't a man more unpredictable or aggressive than my dad. My little brother Johnny drowned when he was two, my ma died the day my little sister was born. That left Alfie, Fred and little Rosie, but they've been sent to the countryside. They've ended up with two misers, so if I don't send money every week, they don't get fed."

He runs a hand through his hair and looks unsure. "Were we having a contest? Did I win?"

I sit motionless in the tunnel as bombs fall above ground. They are falling once again – it's unbelievable how quickly you get used to something so shocking.

"So that's why you sell sleeping places," I say. "That's why you want to earn as much as possible storing luggage at Old William's…"

"Oh please." He sounds irritated. "Don't go getting ideas about me being all noble. Yes, I send them money, but I keep most of it for myself."

"But you don't buy food with it."

"Nah. I'm saving. When the war's over, I'm off."

"Where to?"

"One-way trip to America."

The instant he says it, I can picture it. Jack boarding a shiny ship as big as a city. He stands at the railing. The saltwater flies around his ears, nothing but waves on the horizon.

"Then what?" I ask. "In America."

"Over there, it'll be up to me. If I stay here, I'll be a beggar my whole life. As soon as I open my gob, they know enough. But in America, anything's possible."

I shake my head. "Not anything."

"Oh no?"

I swallow. "Maybe your accent wouldn't matter there. Or what your dad does. But being lame does matter. Being lame is a problem everywhere."

"Don't be such a whinge," he says calmly. "Did you know President Roosevelt had polio too? It's true. The most powerful man in America uses a wheelchair."

"You're making it up."

"I'm not. One of my mates is a paperboy. He knows everything. Roosevelt doesn't advertise the fact, but both his legs are paralysed. And nobody cares."

I stare at him, and he smiles back.

Nobody cares… I suddenly feel the rolling waves. Just picture it. The bow of a shiny ship cutting through the ocean. My hair blows around my face. The sky is a blue dome…

There are footsteps in the tunnel. Two silhouettes approach us, and we hear Quinn's voice echoing in the darkness.

"I can't do anything about it. There's going to be four of us from now on. Jack, a new customer for you."

She stands there with her tiny waist and her dark curls, and of course everyone looks at her immediately.

"You were supposed to take Robbie back," I say curtly.

"Change of plan. He's going to take part in real life here. He's had enough of the baker's wife's big feet."

"Mum agreed," Robbie says. He begins to giggle. "I think she wanted to hear more about the milkman's baby. But the neighbour didn't want to tell her with me there."

While he quickly lays his bedding down next to Jack, Quinn comes to sit with me.

"I couldn't help it," she whispers. "Robbie said he needed to sleep next to you tonight. He was almost crying."

"But why on earth?"

"He told me about that iron monster you had to lie in for weeks. First, the monster helped you breathe and now he's doing it. That's what he said. You share a bedroom at home, right?"

I nod.

"Well, he's convinced that you need him, that you'll forget to breathe in the night otherwise."

I look at my skinny brother and sigh. "He's mad."

"He's sweet," Quinn says. "He wants to be with you…"

I see her face and know she's thinking about Sebastian. She's wearing exactly the same expression that he had just before we left. She's breaking inside but she's too well brought up to let it show.

"Oh yes!" Quinn cries. "I almost forgot. I was on the subject of men being rotten scoundrels. Listen to me, Jack—"

"Actually," I say, "we've moved on to something else. We're having a competition to see whose life's the most miserable."

Jack looks up and for a moment I feel the rolling waves again.

Robbie is sitting next to him, holding a toy aeroplane. They've been poring over something together, a crumpled piece of paper with pictures of bombers.

"Quinn ain't a contender," Jack says. "Look at her. The most miserable life? She'd never win that one."

Quinn smiles. "No? What was your entry then?"

"Two dead 'uns, one loony and a bombed house."

I clench my hands. He hadn't told me about his house.

"Hmm," says Quinn. "What do I have to offer? Around a hundred lunatics who go back to the time of William the Conqueror, parents made of stone, a brother who'd rather be a Nazi than part of our family, and then there's me… I spent my last night at home with the stable boy. My father caught us together at seven in the morning, by nine I'd packed my belongings and left the house." She yawns. "But more on that another time. I'm really falling asleep now. Goodnight, everyone, sweet dreams…"

17

I sleep through the whole night.

We don't wake up until the platform guard shouts out the all-clear for above ground. Without looking at each other, we fold up our blankets. We stink, my mouth is dry, I need to pee but refuse to use that awful bucket.

But everything pales into insignificance compared to what Quinn told me yesterday.

Once we're outside, walking through the drizzle, on our way to warm porridge and a toilet with strips of newspaper, I tug at her arm.

"Tell me then."

"About what?" she asks innocently.

I slow down. "The stable lad of course!"

Her eyes twinkle. "All right, but first you tell me. What's your imaginary version of events?"

"He's the love of your life and now you're pregnant. You're too young to get married in England but it's allowed in Scotland. You'll have to run away to Gretna Green together!"

"Gosh!" She begins to laugh. "Everyone always gets pregnant in your imagination. It was earlier this week, the night I spent with Dick, so it'd be a little too soon to know. But I'm definitely not pregnant because we didn't have intercourse."

I frown. "We don't have a dictionary at home, remember?"

"Oh yes, sorry. I mean, we haven't had sexual intercourse. No sex."

I feel my cheeks turn bright red. I quickly look around to make sure no one heard.

"Are you embarrassed?" she whispers. "Do you feel uncomfortable talking about this?"

I nod.

"Should I stop?"

I hesitate. Then I shake my head.

Nobody I know talks about these kinds of things. Books are always frustratingly vague. Before I got ill, I was still a child. And now not a single man gives me a second glance, so my mother's had no reason to explain the facts of life to me.

"I kissed him," Quinn says, "not because he's the love of my life but because I wanted to."

I stare at her. My hands glow.

The rain begins to fall harder now; people open umbrellas and hurry homewards. Quinn and I stand under a little archway between two houses. The rain whips down in windy gusts, but I don't feel the cold.

"Don't you ever feel that?" Quinn asks. "That desire to kiss somebody? Dick is funny and he's got sticking-out ears and he stutters when he has to speak to my parents. But when he's brushing a horse in his vest, he's unbelievably sexy…"

I've never heard a girl call anything sexy before.

My head spinning, I think about yesterday when I was lying in bed and running my hands over my skin. Is it possible that Quinn does that too? That she sometimes feels like doing that too?

"I'll be honest about it," she says calmly. "It does help that Dick is a stable boy. I knew my parents would go mad when they caught us."

"You *deliberately* got caught?"

She shrugs. "Something had to give. After Sebastian left, the atmosphere was as cold as ice. They knew there was a second rebel in the house – me. They didn't let me out of their sight for the whole year. I could only breathe when I was in the stables with Dick, helping with the horses."

"Are your parents mean?" I ask. "Do they beat you? Or lock you up? Or not give you enough to eat?"

She shakes her head. "That's what makes it so hard. Everyone else finds the lord and lady *so* kind. And I'm the ungrateful, good-for-nothing daughter…"

"But why?"

"I don't know! Because it's the way I am." She pinches her arm, looks at it and says quietly, "This. This is who I am…"

The rain gushes down around us. Little streams run across the pavement; the street is almost flooded.

"I swear," she murmurs, "I do my utter best to be good. But there isn't just one right way to live. The world is huge, so much bigger than my parents think. Their blinkered view of life drove me crazy – I suffocated in their stuffiness. It made me sick the way they forbade things just because nobody had ever dared do them before..."

Cold rain lashes our faces. Her dark hair hangs in wet coils around her face, her skirt is stuck to her body, but it doesn't matter. I've never seen anyone so full of life. Every muscle in her body longs for movement; she's so healthy, it's hard for me to look at her.

"It's the twentieth century," she cries, like she's standing before a room full of people rather than alone with an invalid in the pouring rain. "I want to be able to kiss someone if I feel like it. But I never want to have to get married! I want to wear baggy trousers and a stunning ball gown. I want to do a job that matters and travel the world on my own. And yes, I happen to be a girl but that doesn't mean I only want half a life!"

Her cheeks are red, her eyes shine. I haven't even spoken but I feel out of breath.

"Now your turn," Quinn says. She spreads her arms. "Tell me! What do you want?"

I shake my head silently.

"What? You don't want anything?"

"Nothing out of the ordinary." I stare at the ground. "I'm not, erm, as modern as you. I wouldn't need much..." I gulp. "But who's going to want a girl with a leg like this?"

I stick out my special shoe and we both look at the stiff leather, the thick sole, the long row of laces.

"You're mad," she says indignantly. "Why does it always have to be about men? You wanted to be a writer, didn't you? A leg like yours won't stop you doing that!"

I clench my fists. "And what if I did want a boyfriend? You say the world's bigger than your parents think it is. But as soon as an invalid starts talking about men, you say, 'Go and write novels.'"

I take a step back.

Rain drips down my neck, the pavements are glassy, there's nobody left out on the streets.

"I know I'm skinny and crooked. But I see the inside of my head every day and I'm not lame in there! I have feelings just like everyone else. I know I'm only fourteen, but I also want to… I mean…" I stop in confusion. "I also feel like, erm…"

"You mean you also feel like kissing a sexy Dick?"

The moment she says it, she slaps a hand over her mouth.

For five whole heartbeats I hear only the racing of my own blood, and then I break out into a fit of giggles.

"I didn't mean it like that," Quinn cries. She begins to giggle too. "You know I meant Dick the stable boy. I meant a sexy *man*, honestly, I did!"

We try to stop laughing but can't.

We walk home through the pouring rain, stopping from time to time because we're laughing so hard we can't breathe.

We pass dripping sandbags and extinguished incendiary bombs, and in a couple of hours' time I'll have to stand in that queue again. But right now I feel as alive as Quinn.

"It's idiotic though…" She takes a deep breath. "There's so much stuff we never talk about."

I start to laugh again. "But you talk about everything."

Her expression is serious for a moment. "No, really. If the world were a tea party, we'd only talk about cucumber sandwiches. No one would mention freshly baked scones or lemon cake or jam tarts or iced biscuits, or shortbread, apple crumble –" she takes a deep breath "– big bites of sticky chocolate pudding…"

"Stop it!" I cry. "You'd have to wash your mouth out with soap and water for that at our house."

And so we walk along in the rain, laughing like six-year-olds – or maybe like twenty-six-year-olds, all grown up and in a world that is much bigger than our parents think it is.

18

The rain has stopped, our fits of giggles too. I'm on my own again like I was so much of last year. But today I'm not sitting in the corner with my notebook on my lap, longing for another world.

I've stopped living on paper.

I calmly buy a ticket from the machine because I know how to now. The people who are going to sleep in the Underground tonight won't be allowed in for ages, but I am. The platform feels enormous without people lying on blankets.

As I whoosh through the darkness in a swaying tube train, I try to figure out what I'm going to say to Sebastian. But I keep hearing whispers to the rhythm of the hurtling wheels: *I'm going to sleep in the tunnel tonight! I'm going to sleep in the tunnel tonight!*

I'll see them again this evening, Quinn and Jack. In our little strip of no-man's-land under the ground.

I'd expected it to be difficult to shake Quinn off today, but it was astonishingly easy. I can still hardly believe it.

Over breakfast, my mother talked about her voluntary work in the rest centre, where they were putting up the people who had lost everything. And then Quinn cried, "Oh, please can I help you? I can fold blankets and hand out soap or just scrub floors…"

Blimey, how my mother perked up. Nobody in our family has ever suggested that I go and help out there. It's not a place for invalids. But now there was a shiny, healthy candidate at the table.

"We could definitely use a spare pair of hands," my mother said. "But it's unpaid work."

"Well," said Quinn, and I thought about the treasure trove of jewellery under my bed. "You know what, that's not an issue."

After that they completely forgot about me. My father was asleep upstairs after his shift. Robbie rushed off to play with a friend after eating his porridge. I only had to wait for Quinn to put her trousers back on and go off to the rest centre with my mother and my mission could start.

*

I get off at South Kensington station. I ask a kind-looking grey-haired lady the way to the Albert Hall. From there, I know I can find Sebastian's red-brick building.

I walk along the spotlessly clean pavement, past the fancy terraced houses plastered white, and try to act like my heart isn't pounding in my chest. My summer dress and cardigan are shabby; my mousy hair hangs the way it usually does, in a side parting to my shoulders.

Is fourteen the absolute worst age to be? Or is this me for the rest of my life? Skinny, flat-chested and shy?

I'm relieved when I find Sebastian's building. But the feeling is short-lived: the porter refuses to let me in. When I was with Quinn, no one questioned my right to be there; today I'm nothing but some poor person from a different world.

Now I'm really at my wit's end. The porter's grey moustache and jowls make him look gruff. I take a step back and have to do my best not to burst into tears. I'm angry at the snarling porter, but even more so at myself. Of course they're not going to let an unchaperoned, scruffy girl into a student's bedroom.

I'm about to turn round. Back to the Underground, back to my own part of London where most people are even poorer than me – but then two young men wearing AFS uniforms come in.

If they'd been regular students, with colourful ties and natty suits that cried, *This is the best time of my life and later I'll be prime minister*, I never would have dared. But volunteer firemen exist to help people – you can never be scared of them.

"Excuse me!" I call out before I can change my mind.

The lads stop. They are wearing uniform jackets with a double row of buttons, broad belts high on the waist and metal helmets. My father has the same kind of helmet for his ARP watch, shaped like half a football but with a brim. It's hard to imagine that a thing like that, balanced high on your head, would really protect you from bombs.

"Do you know Sebastian?" I ask in a strange, hoarse voice. I clear my throat. "Lord Sebastian, I mean…"

They give me an amused look but don't reply.

"He lives on the second floor, there on the right. He's got a gramophone and a green pair of pyjamas…"

The boys begin to grin.

"I don't want anything from him," I hurry to add. "Not money or a baby – I just want to talk to him. I was here yesterday with his sister, but now the porter won't let me in…"

The tallest of the two lads begins to laugh and takes a bow. "Eccentric visitors are always welcome." He casts a glance at the porter. "Stiff old Georgie never budges, but we can slip you in on the other side of the building. Sebastian's probably practising in the Union. Follow me!"

I can't believe they're really going to help me. They haven't said anything about my dress or my leg but are just taking me to Sebastian. I walk between them along the broad pavement as quickly as I can. Yesterday I'd seen the red-brick building from the courtyard garden; now we're walking around the outside.

I glance at the profile of the tall boy next to me. He has a pointy nose and a wry mouth, and I'd like to ask him whether life's easier when you talk like the people on the radio. Whether anything can ever bother you when you know you always have the best manners of everyone present.

We enter through an enormous wooden door, and I squint my eyes. The dimly lit hall smells of alcohol and cigars. My feet sink into the plush red carpet and somewhere in the distance I hear music.

We follow it up a flight of stairs, down a corridor, and the music gets closer and closer. The boys open a door, and the notes wash over me like the smell of freshly baked scones and lemon cake and jam tarts all at once…

In a bright empty room, two boys are playing the trumpet and another one the saxophone. A fourth is playing the piano, and standing in the middle of them is Sebastian.

He's wearing the same pyjamas and red dressing gown. On his feet are a pair of flowery slippers and tied around his neck is a yellow silk scarf. I look at it for a moment, but all I can do is listen to his voice, which is warm and fluid and makes your skin tingle without you being touched.

I stand there in the doorway, and I know that Quinn was right: it's crazy only ever talking about cucumber sandwiches.

"Can you stop the racket for a mo?" the tall boy next to me asks, even though they haven't finished what they were playing. "A visitor for *Lord Sebastian*!" He chuckles. "This young lady swears she's not after money or an illegitimate baby, so she appears to be an excellent match." He gives me a serious look. "Sadly, I must take leave of you now, miss. It's almost time for our shift."

Before I can say anything else, the boys have left, on their way to the fire station. I watch their black uniforms disappearing down the long corridor and I get goosebumps.

I was blind. I saw two spoiled young men, rolling in money and good manners. Their uniforms were no surprise, because there's a war on: half the population of England's wearing uniforms.

But their uniforms change everything.

In a spot where a bomb has just been dropped, where the flames are licking and raging, where the emergency services are lit up by a hellish light as the next bomber approaches, it doesn't matter what kind of accent you have. When you're racing along in a ringing fire engine in the middle of the night on your way to another fire, it doesn't matter whether or not your family tree goes back to William the Conqueror.

I watch them walk away along the corridor and it's as though I'm looking at ghosts. The shadows of boys who are alive now – but for how much longer?

"Ella?" Sebastian faces me. "Your name was Ella, wasn't it?"

I nod.

"Where's Quinn?"

Yesterday Sebastian was an older brother, now he's a man. A handsome man in a silly dressing gown with stubble on his cheeks and dark eyes.

He looks like the doctor in my stories. The way I'd imagined every hero up to now.

Every paper hero.

But this isn't a story.

"Where's Quinny?" he asks again. "Has something happened?"

"Well," I say, taking a deep breath, "actually it has. She's run away from home with the family jewels in her bag and she's sleeping in the Underground at night. She's wearing trousers and she never wants to get married, there's a war on and you're the only person who understands her. She's fifteen. She's your little sister. And she misses you."

19

Sebastian looks at the other four boys. "Time for a break. We'll start again in half an hour."

I thought he'd come out into the corridor now, but he stays standing there.

The boy at the piano gets up silently, the three brass players put down their instruments, and one by one they leave the room. Sebastian is given four winks, and I'm given four very polite nods.

"Come in," he says once they've left.

He closes the door behind me and lights a cigarette. As he's blowing the first puff of smoke away, he looks me up and down.

I stand there without moving. I'd expected to be scared. When Jack looks at me, I quiver. But this is the place over the rainbow.

I don't think for a second that any of these students would want to go on a date with me. I don't care if they see who I really am. I don't long for their arms around my waist; no one is saying their sweat smells nice.

It makes everything simple.

At least, that's what I thought.

"Did Quinn send you?" Sebastian asks coolly. "As far as I can recall, the maids back home were rather better dressed."

"I'm not a maid!" I say indignantly. "I'm..." I stop.

The air in here is frosty without the music.

Sebastian raises his eyebrows. "You don't know who you are? That's never a good sign."

"I know who I am," I say in irritation. "But this is about Quinn. Last night I slept next to her in the Underground. Two hours ago, she had a bowl of porridge at our breakfast table and right now she's helping my mother in a rest centre. I've only known her for three days but she's..." I stop again. I shake my head impatiently. "Quinn's..."

I can't.

"Are you suffering from memory loss?" Sebastian asks. "Should I fetch a doctor?"

"Oh, shut up!" I cry. "Just act normal for a minute. Are you a real person or an arrogant clown?"

He begins to grin.

"Do you know why I keep stopping?" I say. "Because I want to say that Quinn's my friend. But I can't get it past my lips. Since being ill, I haven't had any friends. But now I do. And it just so happens that Quinn doesn't give a toss how many frayed edges my skirt has."

"Fascinating," he says. "I was aiming for witty and intelligent, but your take is an arrogant clown. Do you really mean that?"

I give him a stern look. "I just heard you singing. I know you're not a clown."

"I've never heard you sing," he says cheerfully. "But from this conversation I'd very much like to know more about you. Would you care to go for a cup of tea? I could do with one."

*

When we enter the tearoom together, everyone stares. Sebastian has assured me that it's not completely inappropriate for a fourteen-year-old girl to drink tea with a student. He's also explained to me that, at present, it's not possible for him to wear anything other than his dressing gown and pyjamas. It has to do with a bet, but he can't tell me more than that.

Whatever the reason, all the ladies in the tearoom look at him, not me.

I carefully pour us each a cup. The teapot's spout isn't leaky, and the cups have a golden rim. Sebastian ordered carrot cake as well, and as I take a polite bite, I picture the way Jack wolfed down that corned beef sandwich.

"So Quinny doesn't know you're here?" Sebastian asks.

I shake my head, and he sighs. "She thinks I'm a miserable coward. Well, she's right. I am a coward. But last summer she was only fourteen. I couldn't bring her to London with me, could I?"

It's a while before my mouth is empty again. The carrot cake is fresh out of the oven, full of juicy raisins, and it ends up being impossible to take only polite little bites.

"You could have written to her," I say. "Just to her. So that she knew you weren't a Nazi."

"I started a letter, but Quinn's a *girl.* She's stuck there. She'll have to spend years at home still and that's easier if she can join in with the others. If she can hate me together with our parents and Augusta, Violet and Cecilia…"

"Join in with the rest?" I raise my eyebrows. "Quinn?"

He doesn't laugh. His fingers tap the table restlessly. "This catastrophic war… Nobody knows how many will have to die before it's over. But maybe when it finally is, this'll be a country that Quinn and I fit better in."

"What do you mean?"

He lowers his eyes, his face is pale.

"Why do you want England to change?" I ask. "Or do you mean…"

I look at his hand. His fingers quiver and suddenly I feel dizzy.

"Do you want Hitler in charge?" I whisper. "Was Quinn right all along? Are you a trai—"

"Shut up!" he hisses. "I want us to win this war as much as you do. But I hope to God that we never go back to the way things were. You say that Quinn's wearing trousers and never wants to get married. Well, give us a world in which *that* is possible."

His hand is still shaking; he has to do his best to keep his voice down.

"For centuries, we've let ourselves be caged," he goes on. "Men do men's work in men's cages. Women get bored to death in women's cages. There's a golden cage for the rich, a crummy cage for the poor. And then there's a pitch-black corner for everyone who has the bare-faced cheek to want to live in a world without cages."

I see that he wants to shout but I don't understand. "You're a man! You're studying in London and one day you'll inherit an estate. Is your cage really that awful?"

"It's a cage. With bars and a lock."

Between us, on the snow-white tablecloth, there are gold-rimmed teacups and a plate with a few tiny crumbs of carrot cake left on it.

"Do you really think the war's going to change anything?" I ask. "Those cages have existed for centuries. They keep life…orderly." I think about the conversation I had with Quinn on the street this morning in the pouring rain. "It'll be a long time before we live in a world where it's all right for your sort to spend a night with a stable boy…"

"Pardon?" His eyes dart around the room. "Have you lost your mind?"

He sits bolt upright in his chair, blotches appear on his cheeks. Suddenly, there's a vacuum between us. This is what it felt like in the iron lung when the bellows had sucked out all the air.

"I'm sorry," I say breathlessly – I didn't mean to give anything away. "I shouldn't have said that."

He shakes his head. "I don't understand why Quinn…" He stops. "Have you spoken to Dick?" he asks, nervously rubbing his chin. "Is he in London? Did my father fire him?"

"I don't know," I say. "I only know what Quinn told me."

"And that was?"

We stare at each other, and I try to understand what's going on. Quinn saw her brother just once here in London. That was yesterday and I was with them the whole time. She hasn't told him anything about Dick, I'm sure of that.

Sebastian couldn't have known that his sister had spent the night with the stable boy. So why isn't he asking questions about her scandalous behaviour? Why does he only want to know how Dick is?

"I understand," he says quietly, even though I haven't replied. "We won't discuss it any further. That's for the best. But you do understand me then. The life I want is illegal. A criminal offence. That's mad, isn't it?"

I sit there, motionless, as my head throbs. I've got lost somewhere in this conversation and I'm trying to figure out where. What did I say? What did he say?

One sentence pops into my head again. *It'll be a long time before we live in a world where it's all right for your sort to spend a night with a stable boy.*

That's what I said and then he reacted like he'd been caught out.

As though *he'd* done something wrong.

I look at him and slowly my cheeks begin to glow. Now I can feel them inside my own mind: the bars of ancient cages. Locks without keys. Walls.

I try to think, but I don't have the words for this. I want to be a writer, but nobody has ever taught me to talk about things outside my own cage. I feel furious.

I clear my throat and make a decision. I don't give a damn about all those locks and bars. They are adult cages, not ours. Not mine.

The boy before me is simply Sebastian, Quinn's brother.

"Every night," I say quietly, "we sleep in the Underground at Liverpool Street station. You go down the escalators to the Central Line. At the end of the westbound platform there's an unfinished tunnel. We sleep in there, near the back wall, where it's dark and quiet. Will you come and see us there?"

He takes a deep breath. The vacuum has disappeared.

He slowly takes the last cigarette from a flat silver case. "She doesn't want to see me."

"Of course she does. She's furious, but she's your sister. No one knows who's still going to be alive tomorrow. There's not enough time to wait for a different world. She wants to see you in *this* world."

20

Jack isn't in the tunnel.

It's nine o'clock at night but he's nowhere to be seen.

Robbie has been keeping our places in the tunnel since four in the afternoon. I had to sit on the packed platform to save the places for my parents and uncle and aunt.

We've eaten, we've spread out our blankets between the iron girders and we're ready for the night.

All we're missing now is Jack.

"He was supposed to be here at seven," says Robbie. "He told me not to sell the extra sleeping places – he wanted to do that himself."

"An air raid could start at any minute," Quinn says. "He won't be able to get in if he doesn't come soon. I heard the wardens clear everyone off the streets and make them go to a public street shelter or the trenches in the park."

I keep quiet.

I haven't mentioned my visit to Sebastian. And I've stopped saying it's mean to sell sleeping spots – how can I if Robbie's helping Jack, and Quinn is going to pay him for our spaces?

That's if he comes.

Up to now we've been lucky. I knew this already but now I'm properly realising it. Other houses have been flattened; other people got buried under the rubble.

Every night luggage labels are attached to those other people, their injuries scribbled in pencil – it saves time in the hospitals. And when the labels run out, they write what's wrong with you in lipstick on your forehead. My father knows what all the letters mean: an X is for internal injuries; T means you were bleeding so heavily you needed a tourniquet.

Every night those other people are transported to the public baths that now serve as a mortuary.

Not us.

Not yet.

"He must have found himself a girlfriend," Quinn says. "Or a couple of girlfriends. Who knows what a handsome fellow like him gets up to."

"We all know what *you* get up to," I say before I can stop myself.

She begins to laugh. "I know exactly. Today I mopped a floor for the first time in my life. I made sandwiches and set up camp beds and sang songs with a whole group of children…"

"Sounds like a lovely day," I snap.

I look away; she has to stop talking. I need every part of my brain and both my ears to listen for approaching footsteps.

Will he come down the tunnel towards us at last? Or will he stay away?

Is he lying in a dark corner with a girl, or somewhere out on the street with a label around his big toe?

Finally, at ten o'clock, I hear footsteps.

And right after that, "Ouch! Be careful!"

And a minute later, "Watch out, you idiot!"

Jack approaches through the tunnel. Slowly, shakily.

I've no idea what the matter is. Should I try to help him? Of course not. We'd only fall down together.

He almost trips again and I clench my fists. What is he doing here? If he's injured, he needs to see a doctor as soon as possible. But again, he just manages to stay on his feet. He gets closer and closer, and finally he stops.

Quinn, Robbie and I are sitting between the iron girders, and he towers above us. His face and arms are covered in streaks of soot; his clothes are grey with dust. In his hand he's holding a paper bag.

"Bloody hell." He takes a step back. "They're waiting for me. Like a class of bleedin' schoolkids."

He can barely articulate. He takes a dark-coloured bottle from the bag. He pulls out the cork and puts it to his lips.

"Well?" He wipes his mouth with the back of his hand. "Anything happen today? Did Hobble-along pass out again? Did Quinn grope any servants?"

I hold my breath.

"Keep your voice down." Quinn's voice is frosty. "Do you want to be arrested? Public drunkenness is not appreciated in a place where women and children are sheltering."

"Who are you anyway?" Jack asks. He sits down on the ground, facing us. "A stinking-rich tart who thinks she can get away with anything – you must be aristocracy. Well, your behaviour ain't very ladylike, that's for sure."

"You can't speak to her like that!" Robbie whispers indignantly.

"Oh no?"

"Do you want a pasting?" My brother balls his fists. "Apologise to her."

Jack smiles vaguely. "This bloody war…" he mutters. He takes a sip and holds up the bottle. "Port! I've been alive for sixteen years and never tasted port before… Long live the bombs. They crack open the houses like walnuts. Crack, another wall gone. Crack, a cellar open – you don't have to do nothing yourself no more." He begins to laugh. "As long as the bottles don't break!"

I feel my body stiffen.

Quinn sits up next to me and I know exactly what she's going to say. *Don't do it!* I cry out silently inside my head. *Don't ask.*

I don't want to hear this.

Jack sells sleeping spots, he insults Quinn, he makes fun of me – and I'm still sitting here. But that's the limit.

If he really says what I think he's going to say, we'll never be able to see him again. We'll have to report him to the police.

"You're drunk," says Quinn. Her voice is made of steel. "I'd like to think you're talking nonsense. But are you telling us you stole that bottle from a house that had been bombed?"

I clench my hands together – it's too late now.

"Yes," he says smugly. "London's a giant sweet shop. Thousands of houses have been destroyed. But if the rubble's not burning, there's plenty to find in the ruins. Sometimes even a whole bottle of port!" He holds the bottle up triumphantly.

I can't look at him any more.

"We need to leave," I say quietly to Quinn.

She nods and stands up.

"Leave?" Robbie asks. "There's no places left!"

I'm exhausted, my leg hurts, I can hardly stand up. "Mum and Uncle Charlie and Aunty Rita can budge up a bit."

"No, they can't!" Robbie folds his arms. "I was just with them because I was so hungry. It's packed there. The three of us would never fit."

I don't say anything else because he's right.

Every night it gets even more packed in the Underground. More and more people need a roof over their heads, and more and more people don't want to spend the night in the cramped Anderson shelters they have dug for themselves.

The government gave everyone with a back garden a building kit. Big metal plates you could use to build your own air-raid shelter. They would be handy if bombs fell for an hour or so every now and then. But to have the whole family lying night after night in a freezing-cold, damp, pitch-black hole half buried under the ground?

"The last tube will go in a minute," Quinn says. "And we all have a ticket… Maybe there's still space left in another station?"

I stagger. I can smell the alcohol on Jack's breath. I see his dusty workman's shoes a few inches from my own shoes and I can't think clearly.

And then we hear a low rumbling, followed by a soft whistling note.

Above ground, the bombers will be approaching again, the hatches in their bellies opening and bombs whistling down over the city.

But it's not them we hear. Deep under the ground all we can hear is Jack's snoring.

He lies there, collapsed sideways against an iron support. Without his blanket, the port bottle clutched to his chest. His mouth half open, his face in the shadows.

"He's not going to wake up for a while," Robbie whispers.

Quinn and I look at each other. We don't want to sleep next to a thug who loots bombed houses. Just imagine. Your house has been destroyed, you're in shock, you and your family go to a rest centre. And then you come back the next day to gather what can be saved, but Jack and his pals got their first. And they've robbed you of your last remaining possessions.

We don't want to sleep next to him but neither do we want to tramp around the city with our blankets, through packed tube platforms and past crammed shelters.

“If we wake up very early tomorrow morning,” Quinn whispers, “he’ll still be asleep.”

I nod. “Then we’ll report him to the police right away.”

“Well…almost right away. First, I have to make my getaway because my parents will have discovered the jewels are missing by now. The police will be looking for me. So *you’ll* have to report Jack.”

“Glad to,” I say. “I hope they lock him up.”

21

I'm woken up by a shove against my leg. I hear shuffling and squeeze my eyes shut, but then suddenly I'm wide awake.

Something's wrong.

I can't hear the platform guard. Nobody's shouting for us to leave the station. I sit up and see that everyone's still sleeping.

Everyone except Jack.

The bottle of port is still lying there but he's at least fifteen paces away from us. Without moving, I watch him go. *I hope they lock him up*, I said furiously, hours ago. But now I'm not doing anything. I'm not waking anyone up. I'm not shouting, "Stop, thief!"

The silhouette in the semicircular tunnel gets smaller and smaller and I clench my hands together. Is this the last time I'll see him? If he's sensible, he'll never come back. We know too much. There are hundreds of other platforms in London; the city is bulging with strangers to rip off.

But he returns after a few minutes. My heart stops beating.

Of course. After drinking a whole bottle of port, he had to make a trip to the stinking bucket. He approaches, without staggering now.

Do I wake up Quinn? Do I pretend to be asleep?

And then he sees me.

"Blimey, I've got a thirst on," he whispers hoarsely. He sits down. "Got any tea?"

He asks as though nothing's wrong. As though he's not a looting criminal.

I hesitate. We'll be sending the police after him soon. Tomorrow morning's the last time we'll ever see him.

But this is now.

Everyone's asleep except for us. These minutes in the middle of the night are outside of everything. This is the cageless hour.

I get out the thermos flask of tea that's actually meant for the morning and slowly stand up. He's sitting between the girders opposite us, next to all the empty sleeping spots he didn't sell last night.

He smells of alcohol and scorched wood.

I sit down next to him in silence. I unscrew the flask, pour the tea and pass him the little beaker. When he accidentally touches my fingers taking it, an electric shock runs through my body.

His skin is rough and warm, and I feel everything at the same time. I feel that we are both alive, right next to each other, breathing, and as the blood races through our veins, incendiary bombs are flying through the air – and Hitler stands over a map, moving around pawns. And I think of all the months I spent alone in my bedroom. When it was already war but nothing had happened yet. When all the people I knew were afraid that I'd infect them.

At some point during those stretched-out, lonely months, the world turned on its head. When people were no longer afraid of me, I became afraid of them. Suddenly, I understood how things worked. Each body is a bomb filled with spit and snot and sweat. And even a body that has to lie quietly under the sheets causes problems.

For a second Jack has hold of my fingers – and then just the beaker. He thirstily downs the warm tea and immediately asks for more. I pour another cup and hold out the beaker to him, but now he knows where my fingers are and carefully takes it by the rim.

"D'you believe in hell?" he asks out of the blue.

"Er…yes, right? Or I mean—"

He interrupts me. "I always thought those stories were a bit exaggerated. But a few hours ago, I was there."

"In hell?"

"Yeah." He sweeps his hair off his face. I see the soot marks on his arms, cheeks, forehead. "My dad's a nasty piece of work but I still wanted to check on him. See whether he was still alive. So I went back to Silvertown – that's where we live." He clears his throat. "That's where we used to live."

I sit next to him, stock-still.

"I walked through Limehouse," Jack says. "Through Canary Wharf, Poplar, Canning Town. All them neighbourhoods round the docks, packed with warehouses and factories that were targets. Packed with thousands of houses too – flattened now."

He grabs my arm. Sparks dance over my skin.

"It's hell there. Tons of buildings on fire, smouldering away, dripping and hissing with water from the fire engines. And before all the flames have even died down, it's time for the next night of bombings. Badly wounded people are being pulled out of the rubble, men with shovels are digging through the ruins to get out as many hands and feet and legs and heads as they can find—"

"Shut up!" I whisper.

"No," he whispers back. "This is happening right now a couple of miles away. Our city's being wiped out and what can we do about it? Nothing! Because it ain't our war… I'm not allowed to join the army yet and Quinn's not allowed to be a nurse, and we're watching London burn before our very eyes and we've only just started out in this lousy, rotten life…"

He lets go of my arm but I can still feel the sparks. He's a solid lump of flaming anger and I can hardly believe he feels exactly the same way I do: powerless.

"What's left for us to do? Form an orderly queue as we get destroyed?! But how do they expect…" I hear him clenching his teeth; I feel his anger burning. "What makes them politicians think I'm gonna go along with everything if they keep screwing me over the whole time? I didn't choose a single bloody crumb of my life. I ain't got no skills, my dad's a good-for-nothing, my ma bled to death with her newborn baby in her arms, and to top it all, they're letting the whole East End die because poor people don't deserve shelters… Who says it's wrong to sell sleeping spots in a world like that? Who says you ain't allowed to take care of yourself when no one else is going to?"

A tear glides down my cheek but I don't wipe it away. I don't want him to see I'm crying.

I don't have any answers to his questions.

Or just one: if we all thought like that, there wouldn't be anything left to fight for. If no one has any scruples any more, if we're all villains, it doesn't matter who wins.

"Did you find your dad?" I ask gently.

He begins to laugh derisively. "Yeah. He's discovered a pub right in the middle of hell. Typical of him. The whole front's been blown off but they're still serving drinks. There was a sign on the street out front – 'More open than usual'. Dad thought that was hilarious."

"And then?"

He shrugs. "I sat down next to him. He ordered me a pint and I asked how he'd got the money and then he told me. London's a sweet shop, he said. The houses are walnuts and the bombs are nutcrackers. People take their money and jewellery when they shelter, but there's always stuff left behind. So that's his line of work now."

"And you thought..." I swallow. "You thought, *What a good idea. I'll do that too.*"

"They've been screwing me over for sixteen years. Why should I keep following the rules?"

I can't feel the sparks tingling on my skin any more; now I feel them racing through my body. If I was a man, I'd punch him.

"You're not stealing from Hitler," I whisper, "and you're not stealing from fancy rich people. You're stealing from people who've just been bombed!"

He's still for a moment, then lets out a deep sigh. "I tried, I really did. I swear to you. On the way back I passed a house without a roof. It wasn't some hovel, and there weren't any coppers because they ain't got enough people to guard all the bombed houses. So I went inside. The walls creaked and plaster fell. I was walking through some stranger's house…" He clears his throat. "I found a box with a child's silver cutlery set in it. Little rabbits on them. I held the box in my hands and then suddenly I felt sick. I couldn't do it, so I just took the bottle of port and pegged it."

He stops talking and I don't say anything either.

He didn't steal the silver cutlery with little rabbits.

At this moment in time, the world is no bigger than three iron girders. The girder next to him, the girder next to me and the one between us. That's all. His breath, my breath, a war that isn't ours.

"I've got a headache." He yawns heartily. "Even the port has screwed me over."

He lies down, pulls the blanket over his body and closes his eyes.

I stay sitting next to him very quietly. My flowery bedspread is on the other side but that doesn't matter. I'm not sleeping.

I stare at my crooked leg, at the high shoe with all the laces, and hear his voice inside my head. *Hobble-along.*

22

This used to be my school.

I study the old building in the autumn sun, the empty playground without its usual racket. No girls with hoops and skipping ropes, no boys playing soldiers. I try to remember the past fondly, but I can't.

All I can think about is last night. Everything he told me. His fingers on my skin, the feeling that we were the only two people that existed in the darkness.

Yesterday I was sure that fourteen was the absolute worst age to be. But maybe I was wrong.

Maybe it's the beginning of the rest of your life.

I have to control myself, I keep thinking. There's a war on. These aren't the days to be walking along the street with a big grin. These aren't the nights you should long for.

But how can I forget the sparks when they are still twinkling inside my body?

I swing open the gate and go into the sunny playground.

I haven't been here since last year. The summer term had just ended; I waved happily to my friends. We couldn't imagine ever spending long days in our stuffy classrooms again.

And we didn't.

I got ill at the end of August. Then, on 1 September 1939, the war started and evacuations to the countryside began. As my classmates sat on the train and sang songs together, weighed down with gas masks and suitcases, I was stuck in the iron lung and Robbie was quarantined at home.

And now my school's a rest centre. I go in through the double doors and stop. The hall that used to smell of pencil shavings and wet boots now smells of disinfectant and smoke.

It's hell there, Jack said last night. And these are the people who escaped from hell. There are men speaking angrily in a language I don't understand, an old lady with blood in her white hair, lugging a clock and a house plant; half-naked children stare into space, their clothes hanging from their body in tatters.

"Ella!"

There's Quinn, a bright red scarf around her head, its knot jutting out combatively.

"Come with me, I need help."

She pulls me right through the group of angry men, past a table with a stack of forms on it and a laughing toddler.

"I've already trodden on two cockroaches today," she whispers. "And the fleas are driving me mad, but I'll be back again tomorrow. And the day after. They need me. For the first time in my life, I can be *useful*..."

She drags me to the kitchen at the end of the corridor. The windows have steamed up and there's a giant cauldron of water on the stove.

"Look!" She points at a crate of muddy vegetables. "What on earth are those? I can hand out blankets and fill in forms, but now they've asked me to make soup! I can't tell them I've never cooked in my life, can I? They'll find out I'm not a normal person…"

Anyone who hears Quinn say a few words and sees her take a few steps realises she's not a normal person. But I'm not going to tell her this. I quickly get an apron from a hook and go to the counter.

"These are parsnips." I hold up a long yellowish root. "This is a turnip. And you know what potatoes are, right?"

She begins to giggle. "Is that their original shape? They're usually served to me in a gratin, or as fluffy mash, or drowning in butter…"

Not long afterwards we're side by side at the counter. Quinn is peeling potatoes for the first time in her life and I'm tackling a turnip with an enormous knife.

"How did it go this morning?" she asks. "Did the police arrest Jack?"

"Well…" My knife stops mid-air. "To be honest, I didn't report him."

"What? But he'll plunder more houses today then."

"No," I say. "He won't."

We've opened the kitchen window. The autumn sun shines in; thousands of particles of dust float through the bands of light.

I take a deep breath and then I tell her about Jack's father. I tell her about the silver cutlery with little rabbits on it, and the younger brothers and sister he sends money to every week. I feel my cheeks grow warmer and I wish I knew so much about him I could talk for hours.

But once I'm done, Quinn's expression is serious.

"Ella…" She hesitates.

"What?"

"You know Jack only talks to you because he wants something from us? He needs Robbie as an assistant, and he wants me to pay for the sleeping spots. That's what he's after."

It feels like a punch to the stomach.

"Of course I know that," I say frostily.

"Phew. I'm glad he's not fooling you. Because he treats you terribly."

I clench my hand around the knife.

She's standing in the kitchen of my old school. She can't even peel a potato and she's only a year older than me. And yet she's a woman of the world who understands how everything works.

And I'm a pathetic invalid who is happy when some crook talks to me.

"I've seen the way you look at him, you know," Quinn says gently. "And I get it. You've just spent a year lying in bed, you haven't been able to experience much. But that boy's bad news. Do you remember what he told us yesterday when he was drunk?"

"Of course I do," I say. The knife glints in the sunlight.

"And a couple of hours later he tells you about a stupid cutlery set he didn't steal. And then he probably takes his shirt off again and you immediately think he's a hero..."

I can hear the angry men shouting in the distance. Women are talking excitedly, and a baby begins to cry.

"I haven't a single doubt," Quinn says. "That boy will end up in the gutter or in prison. When I'd just arrived, he was useful. But now we're done. I won't be insulted like that, and I don't want to see him humiliate you any further. We're not going to sleep in the tunnel any more."

"He was useful?" I repeat.

She nods.

"And tomorrow?" I ask. "Will you go in search of someone else to screw over?"

I see her stiffen.

"You forget that nobody here *ends up* in the gutter," I say. "We're already there. This *is* the gutter. Sebastian was right, we all live in cages. We can't—"

"Sebastian?" she says, and suddenly I'm silent.

We face each other without breathing.

"When did Sebastian say that?" she asks quietly.

Flecks of dust dance around us. I know I've slipped up, but it's not that bad. Now I'm in control: I know more than she does.

"Yesterday," I say.

"You went back to him? Without me?"

I nod.

"How dare you!"

"I know," I say. "I dared."

"You had no right. He's *my* brother."

"Exactly. He's your brother and bombs are falling. The city's full of people who are grieving someone. So I went to him and told him where we sleep at night."

She's pale. "He's going to come to Liverpool Street station? Did he say that?"

"No. He didn't say anything. I told him about the tunnel and then he was quiet."

Quinn is quiet too. She doesn't look like a woman of the world now, but a lost little girl.

"I wanted to help you," I say. "But you can deal with it on your own from now on. And you can cook your own soup!"

I throw the knife down on the counter, tug off the apron and walk out of the kitchen. Through the long corridors with unused coat pegs, back into the city where the air-raid sirens will soon begin blaring again. All the way back to the platform with the rows of sardines, because I know Quinn won't buy me a sleeping place in the tunnel now.

I came to help her but she's ruined everything. The sparks from last night, the things he told me in the dark – I can't even think about his bare arms now without remembering her words.

You know Jack only talks to you because he wants something from us?

He treats you terribly.

And then he probably takes his shirt off again and you immediately think he's a hero…

There's a war on. These aren't the days you should be walking down the streets with a big grin. These aren't the nights you should long for.

No one's going to fool the pathetic invalid now.

23

For three days, the world felt bigger than usual. When Quinn asked for directions to the hospital, she secretly opened my cage.

When I heard Sebastian singing, it was like a blast of fresh air came in.

And when I talked to Jack in the night, the bars seemed to vanish.

But now I'm back with my family and I can't budge an inch. It's six o'clock and the basket of food is on the platform. Mum takes out the sandwiches, I pour the tea, and my uncle and aunt wait.

"Where's he got to now?" my mother asks, concerned.

I stare at her because I don't know why she thinks Jack will come. He never eats with us, and she's only seen him once – when I'd fainted and he carried me along the platform.

"I'll go and look for him," says my uncle.

At that point I realise they're not talking about Jack, but Robbie.

My little brother's not here.

I'm worse than useless. I've been sitting there on the hard floor, staring at the picnic basket, too blind to notice that Robbie is missing.

"We'll look above ground," my uncle says. He beckons my aunt.

"Ella, you'll check the left end of the platform?" My mother's expression is serious. "And I'll check to the right."

I nod. It's too soon to be really worried. There are all kinds of places for a child to get up to mischief in the Underground. Every evening there are children who ride from station to station just for fun. They play tag in the echoing corridors; they tease the pretty girl who sells biscuits and buns on one of those trays that hangs around your neck. Whenever Robbie's not saving sleeping spots for Jack, he's on the lookout for a bit of adventure.

Except at six o'clock.

Dinner is a must. You only miss it if you're lying bleeding somewhere with a luggage label around your toe.

The platform is packed. I walk along the narrow strip that's still clear. My eyes run over the groups faster and faster.

People are chattering away and eating cold pies. They're drinking cider, burping and cheering when an old lady with an eyepatch wins a card game again.

Dozens and dozens, hundreds of people. But no Robbie.

"Ella?" my mother calls. "Have you already looked in the tunnel where you spend the night?"

"He can't be there, can he?" I respond immediately. "He knows it's dinnertime."

"Exactly. But he's not here yet..."

She continues to wait, and I know I can't do anything about it.

UXB, UXB, UXB, I curse soundlessly.

There's no way of escaping the black hole.

There's no way of escaping the boy I never wanted to see again.

I have to go into the bloody tunnel.

My heart pounds painfully as I check for trains, then lower myself down from the platform edge. I trip over the massive girders in the semi-darkness. As usual, it's hot in the tunnel. The warm, damp ocean of people has started to attract mosquitoes. The complaints are getting louder and louder: we already had rats, fleas and lice here, but now there are mosquitoes under the ground too.

As I feel the sweat drip down my back, I tell myself I'll act incredibly coldly towards him. I won't be fooled by his sob stories. No matter how much money he sends to his family, if you sell sleeping spots and call me nasty names, you're a lowlife.

And then I stop.

I see him sitting there in his vest and it's a few seconds before I can remember what I came for.

"Jack..."

He looks up. For a brief instant I see his face the way it is when nobody's looking. Not a trace of swagger, no indifference in his gaze.

"Do you know where Robbie is?"

"Nope." He stretches out his legs. "But when I see him, he's gonna get a talking-to. He promised he'd be here."

"When did you last see him?"

"Early this morning." He frowns. "He ain't come back for dinner?"

I shake my head. "He's vanished."

We look at each other in the half-light. My hands are shaking. This was the last place Robbie might be.

"He can take care of himself," Jack says.

"I know that!" I nervously wipe my hair from my forehead. "I have to go back."

Jack gets up and grabs his shirt. "I'll go with you."

He comes towards me and stops right in front of me. He calmly begins to button up his shirt, and with each button I find it harder to remember all the things Quinn said to me.

"What are you standing there for?" he asks. "Let's find Robbie!"

"What about those places then?" I point at the empty row of sleeping spots he won't be able to sell.

He shrugs. "Tomorrow's another day. Now we're off to find Robbie and give him what for. Come on, Hobble-along!"

I walk after him in the darkness. He jumps up on to the platform and offers me a hand. Without saying anything he pulls me up.

When we reach my family, my mother's paler than I've ever seen her.

"Robbie hasn't been in the tunnel all day," I say.

My uncle wipes beads of sweat from his forehead. “The doorman upstairs hadn’t seen him. Maybe…”

He stops because Jack has whistled piercingly at the dusty boy who’d been sitting five blankets along from us on our very first day.

The child comes running at once.

“You know Robbie, right?” Jack asks tersely. “I often see you together.”

“Yes, mister.” The boy is wearing a very old jacket a few sizes too big for him and shoes with wooden soles.

“You seen him today?”

The boy nods. “This afternoon, in the queue outside.”

“Did he come in when the gates opened?”

“No, he went to catch monkeys.”

“Monkeys?” my uncle says sternly. “What kind of monkeys?”

The boy begins to grin from ear to ear. “The zoo got bombed last night and all the monkeys escaped! They’re loose in the park now. The paperboy was shouting about it…”

As my family begins to talk frantically, I stay quiet.

I think about London Zoo, at least an hour and a half’s walk from here. I remember those little monkeys with the pink faces. Their worried-looking human eyes surrounded by greyish-brown fur.

Robbie stares at them endlessly each year on his birthday when we visit the ape enclosure. He likes taking a ride on the camel, he’ll give a few peanuts to the elephants, but it’s mainly about seeing the monkeys.

And now the three best things in his life have come together: escaped monkeys, bombs and adventure.

Jack looks at me. "Is he really mad enough for that?" he asks quietly. "Has your brother gone to that park on his own?"

"Yes, I'm sure of it."

A tube train rolls up at the platform. The doors open, passengers file on, but I hardly notice. We're there to shelter, not travel. In a few hours the tubes will stop running and the station will be all ours.

"We have to go to the police," my mother says. "It'll be dark soon and Robbie's there alone…"

At that moment I feel Jack's hand on my arm.

"You coming?" he whispers. He nods at the train about to leave. "We'll find him quicker than the police."

"You want to go to Regent's Park?" I feel the sparks again. They should have gone away for good, but they are fizzing like never before. "The two of us?"

He nods, then grabs some wrapped-up sandwiches from our blanket and quickly pulls me towards the open doors of the train.

"We'll fetch Robbie," he cries as he swishes me into the carriage.

"Wait!" my mother shouts, but the doors are closing.

"Don't worry," Jack calls out through the last chink, "we'll find him!"

And then the doors are shut and the train sets off. Dizzy, I hold on to a metal pole. Black nets have been taped over the windows so we won't be riddled with glass if there's an explosion. In the middle of each net there's a tiny opening you can look through.

As the train accelerates, I see the astonished faces of my family disappear. The packed platform glides past and we zoom into the pitch-black tunnel.

24

Have we lost our minds? Yes, we've lost our minds.

We sit together in the rocking carriage, cramming sandwiches into our mouths.

The commuters ignore us but I can feel the disapproval in their eyes even when they're *not* looking at us. Jack is by far the dirtiest person in the whole carriage. People who've just been bombed out of their slums in Silvertown don't travel by train. Pale skinny girls without a job don't belong here either.

And yet we're sitting next to each other, zooming underneath the city that grows darker by the minute. The sun sets, the dusk deepens, nowhere do any lights flick on. London gets ready for a new night.

And as I chew in silence, I want to shout out, *I have a choice.*

We have a choice.

We're fourteen and sixteen, we didn't start this war and we've no chance of ending it, but for the first time since the bombings began, I don't feel so unbelievably, frustratingly powerless.

We change trains at Oxford Circus and then it's just one more stop to Regent's Park. When we reach street level, panting, the dusk has been replaced by night.

"Right," says Jack calmly. "Your turn now. We're at the park but I ain't got a clue which way it is."

I take a deep breath. We're on the pavement in the dark; trees are rustling next to us. I feel how smooth the paving stones are under my shoes. Just next to us there's a road – that must be it because I see cars driving past. Their headlamps are covered apart from a very thin slit, and they can't go more than twenty miles per hour.

"You've never been here?" I whisper. "You've never visited the zoo?"

"Nah. We don't pay to see animals. Fleas and rats are free. So you tell me, which way?"

I think a moment. Last year I didn't go to the zoo – I was too ill, of course. The last time was two years ago. I'd followed my father through the enormous park without really paying attention.

"First, we have to cross this street," I say because I can remember that. I remember taking Robbie's hand to cross the busy road filled with double-deckers and shiny cars.

Now nobody is holding my hand. We wait for minutes until there are no cars to be seen from either side and then we step into the road.

"Fingers crossed!" says Jack cheerfully. Over recent months cars have crashed into each other in the blackout and run people over every night.

We cross the street together. I know he can walk faster than me, but he doesn't. We step back up on to the other pavement and find ourselves faced with a fence of railings that is taller than us. When cars drive past you can see the metal spikes gleaming up top.

"So this is the zoo then?" Jack asks.

"We're nowhere near yet. This is just the start of the park." I point into the dark. "The entrance is a bit further along."

But when we reach that corner of the park, the gate is shut. I take hold of the iron bars and rattle them, but it's locked tight.

"We'll walk around it," I say. My voice sounds uncertain. "There's another road after this and then the real park starts."

"Sure?" Jack asks.

"Yes."

We walk on through the darkness in silence. Now my eyes have grown accustomed, I can see a faint row of houses on the other side of the street and the edge of the pavement painted white.

We cross the next road and then we find ourselves faced with another locked gate.

"Hmm," Jack says. "I never go to the park. I've got better things to do. But if I understand right, parks are locked up at night?"

"Clearly," I say. I had no idea either.

I rest my hands on the cold bars. We've really lost our minds. Robbie must be back under the ground by now. He knows there are air raids every night. He'll understand that the sirens will be going off soon.

But little *monkeys* have escaped. Real monkeys are climbing the trees in the park right now. Imagine if you could lure one. Imagine you're a nine-year-old boy and you can take a little light brown monkey with human eyes back to the zoo…

"It's your decision." Jack sounds serious. "Do you wanna go back? Or do you wanna go on?"

The cool darkness fills my lungs. High above my head leaves rustle; in the distance a car honks its horn. I can decide.

Back or onwards. I've no idea what "going on" might mean exactly. I only know that I can breathe freely at this moment, that I can feel the wind brushing past my bare legs; I can hear the hoot of an owl. I know that I don't want to hide under the ground for ever.

"Let's go on," I say.

Jack stands beside me and assesses the stone columns of the gate, the fence railings next to it, the spikes on top.

"These railings run top to bottom," he whispers, "but there's two slanting ones here. I can stand on them. So if I help you up first, I'll be able to get over myself after."

It sounds like a good plan until I understand what it actually involves. He cups his hands together and I have to put my foot in them and get a leg up. Then I'm supposed to grab the bars and pull myself up, scrambling over Jack until I can put one of my feet between the iron spikes at the top. And after that I have to jump down into the park.

All of this with one leg that doesn't really work and a dress that was already too short a couple of months ago. With a pair of pants that were last washed three days ago at best. And a boy who hasn't had a bath for weeks.

"Now get your good foot on top of the railings," Jack pants as he clutches my other leg to his chest. "Come on, Hobble-along!"

"Stop calling me that," I whisper angrily.

He staggers but I can hear him chuckle. "Bother you, does it?"

"Yes."

"I don't mean it unkindly, you know."

I hold the railings with one hand and rest the other on his head to keep my balance. My arms are shaking.

"That's what our neighbour always says," I whisper. "After he's given his wife another black eye."

There's a pause. My heart races, my fingers seek support in his coarse hair, and then I feel him nod.

"I promise," he says, out of breath, "that I will treat you with the greatest respect. Would you like me to start right away? Or shall I keep my hand on your thigh until you're finally on top of those railings?"

25

My cheeks are burning, my legs are shaking, I came within a hair's breadth of being skewered by the spikes on the railings. We've gone to a lot of trouble to climb into a giant cage, and yet I feel like I've finally escaped.

It's colder in the park than on the streets. I pull the sleeves of my cardigan over my hands and shiver. We make our way along the path, step by step, in the pitch-black. Leaves rustle, there are scuffling sounds everywhere and the air smells of damp earth.

And then a cloud slides away and we see the moon.

The world becomes full of shadows and a soft, shimmering light. The park is enormous. A wide path stretches out palely ahead of us; a silvery-grey barrage balloon floats above us. It hangs motionless in mid-air, tethered between heaven and earth.

Jack swears.

"What's the matter?" I ask. "We can finally see something!"

"Exactly. That's what the pilots are saying now too." And then he shouts, "Robbieeee!"

I'm so startled I almost fall over. "Where? Where did you see him?"

"I didn't," Jack says. "I'm looking for him."

"You could've warned me you were going to shout out, you idiot," I snap.

"Oh really?" He stops. "So why are *you* allowed to insult *me*?"

I sigh. "I can't help having a limp. But it's your fault you act like an idiot." And then I begin to shout too. "Robbie! Robbieeee!"

We walk through the empty park, side by side. We shout his name and then stay quiet to listen for a response. I'm terrified people will fetch the police because two halfwits are making so much noise between the trees after dark. But the park is gigantic and nobody hears us.

Robbie doesn't either. Each time we stop and wait for a reply, there's silence.

"Maybe he's gone already," I say after a lot of walking and shouting.

Jack sighs. "Long gone. He'll be safe and sound under the ground by now. He'll have got hungry and now he's nice and warm in the tunnel."

I stop because suddenly the whole world begins to wail. All this time I've avoided thinking about it, but now it's happened. The air-raid warning has gone off.

We freeze. We listen to the ghostly sound coming at us from all sides. I put my head back and see that the clouds have disappeared. Thousands of stars twinkle in the deep blue sky. Does the hair-raising wail travel into space? Does somebody out there know we exist?

Or maybe we'll have stopped existing in twelve minutes' time.

After one minute, the sirens stop and we look at each other.

"We'll never get back to a shelter in time," says Jack.

"No."

"Do you wanna give it a go?"

I take a deep breath. And then I shake my head.

"Do you wanna die?" he asks calmly.

In a flash I think back to the whistling bomb of… When was it? Not even a week ago. I heard it whistling above our house and I thought, *I don't care. Just do it.*

Now I'm here. Another eleven minutes and the planes will arrive. The dark air smells of grass and dewdrops, above my head stars are twinkling, and for the first time since my weeks in the iron lung, I'm certain.

"No," I say. "I don't want to die."

I stretch my arms towards the sky and think back to yesterday morning in the pouring rain when Quinn asked me if there was anything I wanted. Now I know. It's so simple.

I want to go on.

I want to know what's going to happen next. And after that. And tomorrow.

"It's never boring hanging out with you," Jack says. "I'll admit that." He takes my hand and pulls me towards a large patch of grass. "If you wanna stay outside during an air raid, you'd better do it properly."

We walk right into the middle of the big lawn. And then we stand there, waiting. Another nine minutes to go. Maybe eight.

He's still holding my hand, and it feels like I'm made up of nothing other than breath and sparks.

Seven minutes to go.

For the first time, I start to understand soldiers. Why fit and healthy young men are prepared to go to war. Not because they want to die, but because they want to feel alive.

Six minutes.

"It ain't likely I'll die," Jack says suddenly, "nor you. But if it does happen…make sure my little brothers and sister know, won't you?"

My blood races. I let go of his hand because it's impossible to talk to him while feeling his skin.

"Where will I find them?"

"Beechwood Lane…" He stops. "You have to write it down. You mustn't forget it."

"I don't have any paper on me."

He looks at me. Five more minutes. "Why'd you tear up that diary?"

The world spins. "What? But you weren't there!"

"I was. I couldn't let you walk round the station on your own. It was the middle of the night, so I followed you. Believe me, London's full of bad people…"

"Oh really?" My voice shakes. "Are there pilfering drunkards in this city?"

He doesn't answer but stares into the distance.

"You just stood there," he says. "All alone on the pavement, bits of paper flying around, and I didn't have a clue whether you'd come back in before the planes arrived…"

"It wasn't a diary," I say. "I wrote about a life that didn't exist."

"Why?"

Four minutes to go. All my senses are primed.

"I was ill. I couldn't go anywhere. That notebook was…" I ball my fists. "It was my ticket to America."

"I'd never tear up my ticket," he says immediately.

"You're saving up for a real ticket. My ticket was fake."

There's a short silence. Three minutes to go.

"Number twenty-two Beechwood Lane," he says then. "If you ain't got paper, you'll just have to remember. That's how I do things. You get a good memory when you've forgotten half the letters."

Another two minutes.

He repeats the address for me. He tells me the names of the people his brothers and sister are living with and makes me repeat everything. And again. And again.

And then we hear a gentle rumbling in the distance.

"Here they come," he whispers.

26

The wind blows through my hair; my lips are dry. Jack is standing right next to me on the large lawn. My old life has been torn up; I want to know what's going to happen next.

The rumbling grows louder, the air shimmers.

One by one the searchlights flick on. It's like some giants are playing a game. Like they've gone camping together and are shining their torches up into the night.

The powerful beams sweep the heavens. They cross high in the sky and blot out all the stars. And then the sweeping game stops: *gotcha*.

I hold my breath.

A dark swarm of bombers has been caught in the light. They are flying in formation and approaching the city. The roaring of their engines vibrates in my belly. They are getting closer and closer, and I can't think straight. I know I should be afraid, but the droning feels like excitement. It penetrates deep into my body, and I want it to go on.

At that moment the anti-aircraft guns start firing. Across the whole city it sounds like the giants have collected hundreds of pans and are furiously drumming on them, pounding away excitedly at lightning speed. Shells explode in the floodlights.

Everything shudders but the dark formation flies on undisturbed. And then the bombs begin to fall.

Now the giants have a new job: they scrape their nails over a blackboard all at the same time. Whistling and screaming, the bombs come down.

A brief instance of nothing.

And then they explode.

After ten seconds, I can't imagine there was ever a time before the bombs. The explosions are ear-splitting, the ground quakes, there are flashes of light and flames, smoke rises up to the moon.

Breathless, I look at Jack. His face is lit up by the flares attached to parachutes that are being dropped by the planes. His eyes reflect the green-and-white flames; every muscle of his body is tense.

And then I think about Robbie.

From the moment the sirens began, it felt as though Jack and I were the only living beings on earth. It was us and the bombs. We defied fate; we challenged Hitler. The rest of the world was safe underground.

But where is Robbie?

He's bound to be back in the tunnel long ago. He must be. But what if… My mouth is dry. What if he's still outdoors? If he's been walking around the park all this time and didn't know what to do when the air-raid warning went off.

Out on the street you can't stand and watch the bombs. As soon as the sirens begin to blare, the wardens send you to the nearest shelter. But here in the park there aren't any wardens. Nobody has to be rescued in this cage.

Except for tonight.

"We have to get out of here!" I shout.

For the first time since we heard the rumble of the planes, Jack turns his face to me. I see in his eyes that he'd forgotten the rest of the world too. It's mad how the most real thing in your life can feel completely unreal.

"This is going to go on for hours," I shout. "We can't stay here, Jack!"

He seems to wake up. He runs his hand through his hair and looks around. The ground shakes beneath our feet; in the distance I can hear the drone of new planes.

"There's gotta be a shelter in the zoo," he cries. "Come on!"

I hadn't even thought of that. Every department store, every hotel, every large building has its own shelter.

"Maybe Robbie's there too," I shout.

I see that Jack has heard me, but he doesn't reply.

As the searchlights hungrily sweep the sky, we begin to run. Stabs of pain go through my leg, my ankle gives way, my body is stiff from the cold. The fairy-tale feeling I had fifteen minutes ago, the crazy excitement that came afterwards – both have vanished.

Now there's only panic.

Panting, I stagger on as Jack runs next to me. I want to shout that he should go on ahead, he can leave me, but I don't manage.

As soon as there's a pause in the explosions, I hear the jingling bells of fire engines and ambulances. I've no idea which direction they're going. I only know that the planes keep coming from the east. First, they fly over the docks, and that's where the most bombs are dropped.

Maybe we'll be lucky.

"Come on!" Jack shouts. "We have to—"

His voice breaks off.

The giants are scraping their nails down the blackboard; the screech is deafening.

And then it stops.

I'm back in the iron lung. I must be because I can't breathe. The bellows have sucked out all the air and there's nothing left.

Without air, the world is empty.

Everything collapses without sound.

27

I'm lying on the ground.

It's pitch-black. I can taste earth and blood. Warm tidal waves gush over me, sucking at my clothes and blowing sand and gravel through the air. I lie flat on my belly and still it feels like I'm falling. I claw my fingers into the grass to have something to hold on to and I press my body to the ground.

And then the bellows stop, and the pounding waves stop, and I can stop thinking.

Far away I hear a voice calling my name, but that doesn't matter.

The ground feels hard and soft, my head feels warm and cold, the sea rushes in my ears.

"Ella!"

The voice comes closer and then I feel hands on my body. They turn me on to my back. Warm fingers wipe my nose and lips.

"Bah," I mutter sleepily. "Your hands are dirty. You never wash them."

And then my head clears. Grit stings my eyes, I spit out soil, my knees are burning. "Jack! That was a bomb…"

"Yeah." He clears his throat. "Just far enough away. There's an impressive crater in the grass." He wipes my face again. "See if you can get up. We have to get away from here."

It's a while before I can remember where my arms and legs are. I try to move them, and I can. I cautiously sit up.

"Are you wounded?" I ask.

"A few grazes." He rubs his lower arm. "That's all."

I look at his arm and see something shining in the moonlight. I grab him and his skin feels sticky.

"You're bleeding!"

"It's nothing. A little cut. We just survived a bomb…"

Everywhere around us, outside the railings of the dark park, I hear bells ringing and now and then a dull thud. The sky above our heads is momentarily clear. I can smell fires burning in the distance and, closer by, the churned-up soil and damp grass – and Jack.

He's sitting right next to me, looking at me.

I look back. It's almost too dark to see anything, which is why I dare. His face is covered in shadows. We've just survived an explosion.

We sigh in unison, and I see him laugh. And then I kiss him.

His lips are warm and sandy; for a moment I put my hand around the back of his neck, and then I let go.

Without saying a word, I get up and start to run. My lips are glowing, my cheeks are burning. My body has taken an enormous blow, but the blow to my brain was even harder.

I can't believe it.

He didn't say anything, he didn't do anything, he just looked. And then I kissed him.

New planes roar above my head, behind me I hear his fast footsteps, in the distance something comes crashing down. It feels like we'll never reach the end of this path, like we've been going round in circles all this time, like…

"Wait!" I suddenly hear a high-pitched boy's voice cry. "Wait for me!"

My heart somersaults wildly.

"Robbie!" I scream.

A dark shape comes running from between the trees. He flies at me with great speed and then he's in my arms.

He immediately begins to cry. "Ella! I was under a bench… I thought I'd have to stay there all night!" He presses his nose into my shoulder. "I heard footsteps and then I called out. And then I heard your voice…"

I clutch him tight. He's cold and shivering but he's alive.

"What are you two doing here?" he asks with a sniff.

"Ha ha! Very funny!" Jack cries. He only looks at Robbie, not at me. "We were looking for you, you ninny."

"Really?" Robbie lets go of me. "I wanted to catch the monkeys." He wipes his nose on his sleeve. "I almost had one. He was so handsome. He was swinging through the trees, and I went after him and—"

"That's enough," Jack says brusquely. "Tomorrow you'll get a good hiding, but right now we need to shelter. D'you know the fastest way to the zoo?"

"Wow," Robbie cries as he wipes away a few tears. "Are we going to shelter in the zoo? That's amazing!"

Jack sighs and I hold my breath. Now he'll look at me at last, won't he?

But he acts like I don't exist. He talks to Robbie, gives him a shove, and they begin to run along the wide path. And as the bombs start falling again in the distance, I hurry along after them.

28

The rest of the night feels completely colourless. Sounds are dulled; my body is numb with cold. I shove away any thoughts of planes, searchlights and sandy lips.

We've found a place to shelter so we're safe. Thought is no longer necessary.

Robbie knew exactly where the closest entrance to the zoo was. We stood there and shouted until a guard heard us. Every night, men wearing metal helmets patrol the animal enclosures. Firebombs have to be put out as quickly as possible, damaged cages repaired.

A skinny man with a shaggy beard opened the gate for us. Of course we got a good telling-off, and of course we were allowed to take shelter.

Now we're sitting in a chilly pedestrian tunnel with enormous piles of sandbags at either end. Narrow wooden benches are pushed against the wall, there are two smoking oil lamps and men playing cards. There's no tap, so Jack and I stay covered in dirt.

Robbie has struck up an instant friendship with the zebra keeper next to him. As I rest my head against the wall, my eyes shut, I hear the man talking.

After the bombings last night, it wasn't just the monkeys that escaped but also a zebra. The creature galloped a mile through London before they managed to catch it.

Jack is sitting next to me. He still hasn't spoken a word to me.

I clasp my grazed hands together, and without wanting it to, my brain goes back to that dark lawn. I picture us together, looking out for what was to come. The world shimmered, and just waiting there felt like an act of heroism.

I can't believe I took such a crazy risk. I decided to stay outside during an air raid, and I found it exciting too.

I can't believe I forgot at least five times that I was looking for my little brother. There were whole sections of the evening when I forgot to worry.

And I can't believe what happened when a bomb fell and it turned out we were still alive.

I'm silent all night. And so is Jack. And Robbie learns everything, absolutely everything there is to know about the zoo.

When the all-clear is finally given in the early morning, we get to our feet with difficulty. I can feel that I was blasted through the air a few hours ago, my eyes sting, there's dried soil in the grazes on my knees.

We slowly walk through the empty zoo. The sun has just come up, wisps of mist hang low above the ground, the first trees are getting their autumn colours. A camel stands calmly chewing grass; a brown bear is lying with its head in its paws in a concrete enclosure. Even Jack can't manage to get Robbie to hurry.

Just as we're finally leaving through the main entrance, a taxi stops. The door opens and Quinn jumps out.

"You're still alive!" she shrieks through the quiet dawn.

She rushes to us and tries to hug us all at once. She can't manage because between Jack and me there's space for a whole llama at least. Everyone talks at the same time. Quinn gives Robbie a ticking-off and she wants to hear all about our adventure.

"How come you're here?" I interrupt. "You weren't even in the Underground yesterday evening."

"I was though." Her expression turns serious. "At first I didn't want to go. But if there's a chance of Sebastian coming to see us in the tunnel, I need to be there."

"Who's Sebastian?" Robbie says, but Quinn doesn't answer.

"I went to the tunnel," she continues, "and you weren't there. Your family were beside themselves, but it was too late to come and look for you. The bombing started. So I came right away this morning. I almost didn't dare hope..." She looks at Jack and me and sighs deeply. "That was very brave of you both."

"It wasn't brave at all," I say, annoyed. I'm cold and my muscles are aching, and I want to give the invisible llama a kick. "We were mad. We did something stupidly risky and we never should've."

"Shouldn't we?" Jack's hands are in his pockets. There's blood on his shirtsleeve. This is the first time he's looked at me again. "We found the little rascal, didn't we? Without us he'd have spent the whole night lying under a bench."

"We got completely carried away," I say angrily. "We weren't thinking straight. It's embarrassing."

"I'd do it all over again," he says calmly. "Wouldn't you?"

"Of course not!"

"That's good to know." He shrugs. "Then don't kiss me next time. Problem solved."

Silence follows. I hear birds shrieking in the zoo, a donkey begins to bray, but here on the pavement in front of the zoo, nobody moves a muscle.

Quinn and Robbie are watching like they're at the flicks. They wait with bated breath.

"We have to go home," I say curtly. I begin to walk. "I want to take a bath."

"Can I take a bath too?" Jack asks.

I spin round furiously. "No, of course not!"

"I'm not allowed to take a bath?" he asks, amazed.

Quinn and Robbie start to giggle.

"Oh," says Jack. "You mean I'm not allowed in *your* bathtub." He grins. "Who said I wanted to get in your bathtub? Just imagine it. Now *that* would be embarrassing."

29

Nothing happens for three whole days. Just the war. We know what that means for non-uniformed civilians. We know the rhythm of waiting in the queue and waiting under the ground. We're used to fire in the sky and streets pumped full of water, our shoes crunching over pavements strewn with glass.

I cope with the nights in the tunnel by sticking to the rules I made when I was washing myself in the kitchen at home. After the zoo, Quinn took us back in the taxi. My parents were restrained in expressing their immense relief, and after breakfast my mother boiled a big pan of water. And then they left me alone.

I slowly took off my clothes. I dipped my flannel into the warm water and began to wash. My grazed knees, my bruised arms, my swollen lip, my leg. I saw how thin my ankle is, the way my foot turns inwards, my hollowed-out lower leg. And then I came up with the rules.

Number one. My cage isn't made of iron but flesh. Never forget that.

No matter how the world changes, I will still have a limp. There's only one thing for it – a return to my life on paper.

It's time for a new notebook to write stories in. You don't get blasted through the air very often on paper either.

Number two. No more kissing.

A beautiful girl who is admired by every man can easily step out of her cage and kiss someone when she feels like it. That's called "modern". An invalid who kisses someone out of the blue – that's "pushy".

Number three. Carry on.

I don't want to die; I want to know what happens next. I can think whatever I like, I can write whatever I like, I can feel whatever I like. Nobody can put bars inside my head. That's not everything, but it might be enough.

*

On the fourth evening after the zoo incident, Quinn comes over to me.

"I can't handle it any more," she says. "I'm going insane."

I look up from my new notebook. It's an old school exercise book that was still half empty. There's more light to write by on the platform, but it's also busier. Now everyone's realised we might be sheltering together every night for months, they've started to form clubs. Chess clubs and knitting clubs and reading clubs and a choir that is already looking forward to singing Christmas carols.

It's wonderful but also scary to see how quickly people can adapt. Life under the ground feels almost normal.

But not everyone is coping.

"I'm going insane," Quinn repeats. "It was almost a week ago that you visited Sebastian. It's clear that he's not coming. I have to stop waiting but how do you do that? I hurry here every evening, I look up at every footstep in the tunnel…"

"I really thought he'd come," I say. "I'm sorry."

"Nonsense! It's not your fault." She sighs. "I'm a hothead. Like when I ranted on about Jack, saying he was a scoundrel who only ever thought about money. And a few hours later, there he was, risking his life to look for Robbie…"

I say nothing.

Our bit at the end of the tunnel feels like a no-man's-land. There's a bustle and din everywhere except for here. Jack and Robbie have gone to buy extra sandwiches from the lady with the tray; we're saving their places in the meantime.

Quinn takes my pencil and begins to draw stripes on the girder in between us. Suddenly she shakes her head. "It was much easier to be a rebel back home! I lived on a country estate with a father and a mother and three sisters and shouted my mouth off at everyone. I knew the world needed to change and that felt wonderful."

"You still know that, right?"

She nods but doesn't say anything else. She's thinner after just one week. Her hands are even dirtier than mine.

"Do you know what's so silly?" she says.

I shake my head.

"My parents will never change. We disagree about everything. But I still miss them."

I wrap my arms around my knees. It's warm in the tunnel but my leg is always cold.

"You don't have to choose," I say. "You can change the world *and* miss your parents."

"Do you really think so?"

I nod.

Slowly her face relaxes. She carefully rubs all the pencil stripes from the rail with a finger, like a prisoner ready to return home from jail.

"Are you going back?" I ask, worried. "Back to the estate and your parents and sisters?"

She shakes her head immediately. "Fifteen years of eating stuffed quails and caviar are enough for me." She wipes her dusty cheek. "They need me at the rest centre. Not for a tennis match but for real. It matters here that I exist."

She takes a deep breath and then begins to laugh. "I'm not going home but I do want to tell them I can peel potatoes now, that I sleep on the ground every night and pee in a bucket and the world is even bigger than I thought. They should hear about you and Robbie…and *Jack*."

I don't move.

"Come on, Ella!" she whispers. "You still haven't told me anything. Was it true what he said? Did you really kiss him?"

I look at the floor in silence. Sometime in the future, when the war's over, they'll continue digging this tunnel. Trains will whoosh through and the people in those trains won't have any idea what we thought and talked about down here.

"A bomb had just dropped," I say without looking at Quinn. "Everything was dazzling, the air was thrumming. I forgot who I was."

"I don't believe a word of it," she says right away. "You didn't forget yourself. You forgot the rest of the world!"

"What's the difference?" I sigh. "I've still got a gammy leg..."

"So what? Everyone has something the matter with them. Your thing just happens to be visible."

"He didn't kiss back," I whisper.

She begins to laugh, and I give her a shocked look.

"While all those bombs were falling, you mean?" she says cheerfully. "He didn't kiss back after you'd just been flung through the air, and you were lying there all dirty in a freezing-cold park? You think it's because of your leg that Jack didn't take the time for an intimate embrace?"

"But he didn't say a single thing to me," I cry indignantly.

"And what did you do then?"

"I ran away. Another wave of Heinkels was coming."

Her eyes sparkle. "Tell me. Is there anything you need to know for next time? Like, if you want to kiss him again as the world falls to pieces...?"

"Stop!"

"I know exactly how all the parts of a man work."

"Ugh."

"And I know how everything fits together. Believe me, it's not that simple because you can do it in different ways."

For a second I forget that I don't want to hear this. "What?" I whisper.

She nods earnestly. “In lots and lots of different ways. Really, I’ve seen pictures. I know how the—”

“Shut up!” I cry. “There isn’t going to be a next time. Never again!”

30

On the fifth evening after the zoo incident, Jack comes to sit next to me.

I act like I haven't noticed but I quickly close my notebook. I've brought a candle from home now so that I can write in the tunnel at night.

Jack leans his back against the wall and doesn't say anything.

This is new: him coming to sit next to me, after our night in the park.

But what isn't new: him not saying anything to me.

He shunts his shoe back and forth over the ground. His finger taps the girder.

"I, erm…" His finger stops tapping. "I want to ask you something."

I wait.

"There in the park…" he says, and my heart immediately starts beating faster than it's supposed to.

I quickly repeat the rules inside my head. Number one, number two, number three.

"When we were waiting for the planes," Jack says, "you told me your notebook wasn't a diary. You said it was a ticket to America. And you tore it up 'cos it wasn't real."

I've no idea where this is going.

"We were standing there, waiting. I didn't know if we'd still be alive fifteen minutes later. And suddenly I thought, *Who am I kidding?* That ticket of mine's just as unreal. Even if I could pay for the boat, what am I supposed to do in America? I can't do anything."

He balls his fists. The cut on his arm hasn't healed yet. Now and again the wound starts bleeding again, but he just ignores it.

"I've had enough of being a loser. So I've got a proposition to make. You don't have to pay for the places in the tunnel no more. I'll keep them free for you if you teach me to read."

I sit very still.

It feels like I'm no longer alone in the iron lung. It feels like he's asked if he can come and lie down next to me.

For the first time since that night in the park, I look him in the eye.

"You want me to teach you to read?"

"You reckon it's a poor deal? You want extra money for it?"

"No, it's not that…"

"You think I won't be able to? That I'm too stupid?" He sighs. "I played truant half the time, I didn't pay attention. I think it's 'cos of that. I reckon I could learn."

For five days I've acted as though the sparks weren't there. I repeat the rules to myself – but "You mustn't teach Jack to read" isn't one of them. And as I run through the rules again in my mind, I picture the scene. Sitting side by side in the tunnel, night after night. A candle burning and a book between us.

We'd start with the letters he's forgotten. We'd continue with fairly easy children's books. We'd be able to read all my favourite books together…

I know that this is the spruced-up version. It would be different in real life. In real life he'd probably get annoyed all the time. He'd make fun of my favourite books and accidentally call me "Hobble-along" again.

But still.

"Well?" he asks impatiently. "Will you do it?"

"Yes," I reply.

31

On the sixth night after the zoo incident, we hear music on the platform.

Quinn and Robbie are playing cards, Jack and I have just started our first reading lesson. He actually wanted to keep it secret from the others but that was impossible, of course.

"There's no shame in not being able to read," I whisper. "You don't have to be embarrassed about it."

"I'm not! But what kind of idiot actually asks for lessons…"

"You're embarrassed about *wanting to learn* to read?"

"Yep."

"Loser," I say.

He grins. "Hobble-along."

I see Quinn looking at us. She shakes her head and mouths something silently that looks like "lots and lots of positions" and then goes back to playing cards.

Until we hear music in the distance.

Sometimes people sing together on the platform, and everyone knows the man who's driving London potty with his harmonica. But this sounds different.

The sound swells, and then two figures appear silhouetted at the entrance of the tunnel. The left one is wearing a long dress; the right one has a saxophone.

The music stops for a moment and then the sax begins to play again. Low, warm, honey-like notes roll through the tunnel, echoing around us and making us feel like the war isn't the only thing that exists.

People look up. They stop talking and put down their newspapers and playing cards and knitting.

And then the figure on the left begins to sing. I recognise the voice from the very first words.

"That's Quinn's brother!" I whisper to Jack.

"In the dress?"

"It's a dressing gown."

He sighs. "And Quinn wears trousers. Now it's definite. They're aristocrats."

Sebastian sings the song we heard as Quinn and I left him that first time, cutting across the sunny courtyard garden where the students were lounging in deckchairs.

Earlier this year, when I was finding it hard to go on, when I was still suffering from pain months and months after the iron lung, my mother took me to the cinema. In the middle of the afternoon, just like that, we went to see *The Wizard of Oz.*

And now I hear the song about the land beyond the rainbow again.

Deep under the ground, sheltering from the bombs, I get a lump in my throat as I think of a sky that is simply blue. And after that, when Sebastian sings about dreams that come true, I press my nails deep into my palms. I'm sitting here beside Jack and I'm teaching him to read so that sometime, when the war is over, he can break out of his cage and sail to America.

I look at Quinn, and her face seems to be giving off light.

She's not afraid to throw her arms in the air when she's happy; sometimes she shouts in the pouring rain. There's nothing she doesn't dare talk about, and she kisses stable boys when she feels like it.

But this is a different Quinn. There at the start of the tunnel, there's the boy who understands her better than anyone. She sits listening calmly. Her eyes shine; she's waiting. She's in no hurry to jump to her feet and run to him. This isn't about a single moment; it's about a whole life.

Her big brother is back.

As the last notes from the sax die away, people begin to clap. A thundering applause rolls through the tunnels of the Underground, men whistle, children call out for more.

They do it. They carry on.

I'm sure that Sebastian wants to go to his sister, but when half of London is begging you for another song, you give it to them. If a simple saxophone and a boy in a dressing gown can make hundreds of people forget their worries for a moment, then you sing on.

We sit there listening and it feels like we've been momentarily lifted up above our own lives. We can see everything: the way we plough on day and night, all of us, how brave we are and how we almost break, the way we're different from each other, and the way we'll all talk about these weeks or months or years under the ground for the rest of our lives.

All of us, except for the people who don't survive.

Finally, they're done. I see Sebastian patting the boy with the sax on the shoulder, and then the sax boy disappears and Sebastian comes over to us.

When he's three girders away from Quinn, he stops.

"May I come and sit with you?" he asks.

"Of course," says Quinn. "I'll introduce you to my friends."

And that's it.

They don't fall into each other's arms; they don't even say sorry. They just carry on with life and their faces give off light.

The whole evening I do nothing but look at the brother and sister. I can hardly believe how much they look alike. Quinn tells wild stories about the rest centre. Sebastian talks about the university. His degree has been shortened so that he can join the army next summer.

"Will the war still be on then?" Robbie asks. "That's almost a year away!"

Sebastian is sitting close to Quinn. His silk dressing gown glows in the candlelight; he's the only one of us without dirty nails.

He gives Robbie a serious look. "Hitler has taken over half of Europe. More and more countries are joining him, and he's rigged up an immense war machine. As long as America remains neutral, it doesn't look good for us."

"Nonsense!" Quinn gives her brother a shove. "Hitler doesn't understand anything about the Brits. He thinks we'll all surrender if he destroys our cities. Well, the more bombs he drops on London, the more determined we become!"

Jack grins. "They should send *you* to the front."

"If only," she says at once. "And what about you?"

"Another year and a half. I'll turn eighteen in April '42."

The walls of the tunnel shake; a tube train rumbles in the distance. Deep inside my body, I'm shaking too.

"And will you go then?" I ask Jack. I clear my throat. "Are you prepared to fight, even though this country's been screwing you over all your life?"

I see Quinn and Sebastian giving me a surprised look, but I ignore them.

"Yeah," Jack says calmly. "I'll go."

The conversation continues but I no longer hear it.

All evening I've been sitting next to him. The candle between us has almost burned down to the stub; the notebook with letters in it lies forgotten on the ground. All evening, as I've been looking at Quinn and Sebastian, I've known that Jack's arm is resting beside my arm, that our legs are stretched out next to each other.

And now there's a new milestone in my life. April 1942.

It's so simple.

As a man, when you turn eighteen, if the country says, *We need you*, then you go.

And if you're a woman, you stay behind.

"I'm turning ten next week," Robbie says. He cautiously looks at me. "Ella?" He looks like a skinny little squirrel. "What do you reckon? Are we still going to the zoo?"

"That's a good'un!" Jack cries. "You haven't even had your hiding from the last time yet."

"I have too," Robbie says. "Dad made sure of that. I couldn't sit down for three days."

As Quinn tells Sebastian about our night in Regent's Park, I look at my little brother. He's never asked anything about the iron lung; he's never said anything about my leg. But he waits for me when I can't keep up, and he lies next to me every night. He makes sure I never forget to breathe.

"Mum and Dad won't be able to take you to the zoo," I say gently. "But maybe I can… Although, actually…no. Dad won't want to pay for our tickets."

I see Robbie's face and I want to wrap my arms around him. But he's almost ten. Hugs are only all right when we've just escaped being bombed.

"Do you know what the remarkable thing is?" Sebastian says. "I've never visited a zoo. I consider it a flagrant gap in my education. So what do you say? May I accompany you to the zoo next week?"

I begin to laugh. "Do you really want to?"

"Of course."

"You're going to look at camels in your dressing gown?"

"Let's do the sums… No! From Thursday onwards I'll be wearing utterly boring clothes that are completely appropriate for the time of day."

"On my birthday?" Robbie asks. "Are we really going?"

We nod, and for the rest of the evening, Robbie's face gives off light too.

*

Sebastian leaves just before the last train goes.

"Tomorrow night I'm playing poker with a few friends," he says airily. "But I'd like to return the next evening and sit in the dust with you." He looks at his sister. "What do you think? May I visit you all again?"

I see Quinn's thoughts racing as she searches for a witty reply. One of those understated upper-class remarks that comes naturally when you grow up in a country house filled with dictionaries.

But then her face relaxes.

"Yes," she says. "You may."

As Sebastian climbs back on to the platform, I hear a woman call out to him.

"Hey, Mr Songbird! Do you know 'We'll Meet Again'?"

Of course he knows it. That song is played on every radio, people hum it on the street, in the queue for the butcher's, waiting at the gates to the Underground. It's an optimistic song filled with faith in the future, but that's what makes it so incredibly moving.

When everything's going well, you don't have to hope.

The sax boy has gone, but as he walks along the platform, Sebastian begins to sing unaccompanied:

We'll meet again,
Don't know where,
Don't know when,
But I know we'll meet again some sunny day…

It's the song soldiers sing as they're leaving for war. They sing it at the top of their voices, but everyone who says goodbye to a father or brother or son knows that some people are lucky and others aren't.

Keep smiling through,
Just like you always do,
Till the blue skies drive the dark clouds far away.

I sit next to Jack and think about April 1942.

32

On Robbie's birthday one of us dies.

It's a bright sunny morning. More and more of the trees in Regent's Park are turning yellow and orange; the air is cold and crisp.

We enter through the big gates and Robbie walks around like he's the director of the zoo. He's wearing a new blazer; his hair is combed and his knees have been scrubbed clean. He strikes up conversations with the keepers and, to his great relief, he learns that all the escaped monkeys are safely back home again. It was simple: when they got hungry, they decided they preferred their cages to real trees.

I do my best not to keep thinking about the last time I was here. I also do my best not to think about Quinn and Jack, who are working in the rest centre together this morning. Two extra classrooms need to be cleared and I've no idea how Quinn managed this but Jack's helping her.

I try with all my might not to picture him carrying school benches down to the basement in his vest.

Sebastian and I wander calmly after Robbie, and for an hour and a half the war feels far away. Sebastian is wearing a pale grey suit and a dashing trilby hat. His shoes shine, his freshly shaven cheeks too.

We talk about the weather. The exceptionally warm summer, yesterday's rain, whether it's going to be a bad winter. And then suddenly we're no longer discussing the weather.

"Quinn's hardly stopped talking these past few nights," Sebastian says. "I know everything about her running away to London now."

"Really?" I carry on walking slowly towards the cranes. All the other girls here are still bare-legged; I'm wearing thick woollen stockings and an extra jumper.

"Yes," he says in a serious tone. He clears his throat. "Ella..."

I stop.

"In the tearoom I told you about my cage." He doesn't look at me. "There was a misunderstanding. You mentioned the stable boy and I spoke out of turn. Quinn's told me all about her night with Dick now, and I understand why you mentioned him. You were talking about Quinn, not me."

"Yes."

We stand side by side in front of the civet cats. We carefully study their unusual rows of spots, their pointy noses, their fierce eyes.

"Did you tell Quinn about our conversation?" Sebastian asks. "Does my sister know something she didn't use to know?"

I shake my head and hear a long, repressed sigh next to me.

"Good. One day I'll tell her everything. But when I left home, she was still so young…" He straightens his tie. "Enough about me. Let's talk about you and Jack."

I feel my cheeks begin to burn, and he starts to laugh.

"What a scene," he says, shaking his head. "In the middle of the lawn, in a dark park like that!"

"Yes," I say. I gulp. I feel my cage, I take hold of the bars, I rattle the lock – and then I look Sebastian in the eye. "Jack's handsome, isn't he?"

He stands very still. There's not another person to be seen. Only the cranes and the civet cats can hear us.

His cheeks turn just as red as mine, but then he straightens his back.

"Now that should be forbidden," he says airily, "being *that* handsome."

"Have you noticed his eyes?" I ask. "Dark grey with silver."

Sebastian sighs. "And those shoulders…"

"Have you seen him without his shirt on then?"

He sighs again. "Who hasn't? The chap does nothing but casually lean against the tunnel wall in his unwashed vest."

We both begin to giggle, but then I stop.

"What are you going to do?" I whisper. Now I'm not feeling my own cage but his. I think of the people who have to spend their whole life in an iron lung. Who have to live with other people being in charge of their body. "How are you going to keep going?"

"I've no idea. What can I do?"

"Fight," I say.

He gives me a piercing look. "Is that what you do?"

I don't reply.

I think of the rules I made after that night in the park. I think of the new stories I'm writing; a long, cowardly life on paper.

Without a word, I turn round and begin to walk to the exit.

*

Sebastian takes us home in a taxi and my mother comes trotting out to thank him. Her hands are dripping with suds and she quickly wipes them on her apron.

"Incredibly kind of you, it really is!" she says three times. "Robbie, did you thank the gentleman? Ella, did you—"

She suddenly stops talking. A boy on a bike has pulled up right next to the taxi in front of our house, his brakes screeching.

"A message from the rest centre, missus," he cries, out of breath. "They need you. There's been an explosion."

"That's impossible," my mother replies without a moment's thought. "I was there just this morning. They got through the night all right!"

"A UXB in the basement," the boy says. "Went off half an hour ago."

The edges of the world turn black.

I see details more clearly than before, but beyond that, everything's dark. There are droplets of water on the pavement that have fallen from my mother's hands. A blade of grass is stuck to Sebastian's shiny shoe.

There was an unexploded bomb in the basement.

And that bomb has now gone off.

The boy wipes his sweaty forehead and gets back on his bike. Sebastian, Robbie and I haven't yet said a word, but the instant the boy pedals off on his rickety bike, Sebastian calls after him.

"Are there any wounded?"

I don't recognise his voice.

"Yes," the boy shouts back over his shoulder. "That's why we need you."

He flies round the corner and for just one moment we stand there in no-man's-land. Above our heads we hear the dull thuds of a carpet beater, specks of dust whirl in the sunlight. My woollen stockings itch.

"I'll get the first-aid kit and a few sheets," my mother says tersely. "I don't know what'll be left of the place. Ella, you stay with your brother."

"No," I say.

She doesn't hear; she's already rushed back inside. When she comes back out of the house two minutes later, Robbie and I are sitting in the taxi. Sebastian holds the door open for her. He jumps in last of all and the car sets off the moment he's closed the door.

Robbie, my mother and I are sitting on the back seat as Sebastian is thrown around on the folding seat facing us.

"You were supposed to stay at home," my mother whispers fiercely. "You're only going to get in the way. And what if another bomb goes off…"

I clear my throat. "Quinn and Jack are there."

I can't look at Sebastian's face. I took a quick glance a moment ago and it felt like looking in a mirror. A mirror without a back, one you're sucked into and disappear.

These are the minutes when we don't yet know.

Outside the window, I see people walking in the sun. I hear double-deckers hoot their horns, we pass one of those massive red pillar boxes like the one Robbie jumped off the other week, his arms spread.

That whole morning I'd tried not to think about Quinn and Jack. I was jealous. While I was walking through the zoo on a clear day, they were laughing and bickering as they lugged school benches down to the basement.

They didn't ask me if I wanted to help. I could have opened doors for them, I could have wiped away cobwebs or tidied up the last sticks of chalk.

But they didn't ask me to do anything, and all morning I pictured them as I looked at camels and owls and cranes. I run through those imagined scenes of laughter again.

Jack in his vest, Quinn in her men's trousers, the red scarf around her head. I study the images again and this time I add a crucial element to the story: a UXB in the basement.

I know that basement storeroom where they kept the chalk, new board rubbers and broken chairs. I know exactly how the brick stairs from the door in the hall turn as they go downwards. I remember the smell of the damp walls.

One single detail can now affect everything.

Who was carrying the front of the bench, who the rear? Who turned the corner first? Did the UXB explode at the first vibrations on the stairs? While they were panting as they manoeuvred through the basement? Or when they were both standing right next to the bomb and dropped the bench on to the bare floor?

33

From a distance I see two fire engines, an ambulance and a throng of spectators. My hands are freezing. As soon as the taxi stops, we scramble over each other to get out.

I had expected chaos, noise, crackling flames, screaming.

Now all we hear is the tinkle of broken glass being swept up.

They're sitting in little groups, spread out across the schoolyard. Children with scrapes and grazes, silent old men, women covered in dust.

The school building is still standing. Its panes of glass are broken; there's an awful hole in one wall. I can smell a faint whiff of gas but can't see any fire.

As quickly as I can, I scan the people in the schoolyard. No red scarf with a knot on top. No messy hair and a torn shirt.

And then I see three dark grey blankets.

A semicircle on the pavement in front of the school has been left clear. They lie there next to each other. Three long shapes covered in blankets.

Sebastian pushes the spectators aside and walks right up to the blankets. Without saying anything, I follow him.

He doesn't ask the firemen who are standing in front of the door anything. He ignores the women who have been working here for weeks. He goes over to the blankets, and I don't shout for him to stop. I don't want him to leave this task to anyone else.

He doesn't hesitate as he pulls up the corner of the first blanket. I know he doesn't feel brave. I know he's not thinking. He can't do anything else.

I stand next to him because we need to know.

We stare at the face of an old lady with white hair. Sebastian quickly puts the blanket back.

The firemen come over to us, but Sebastian is already lifting up the second blanket.

A girl with long plaits and a throat covered in blood. She looks like Dorothy from *The Wizard of Oz*. The girl who sings about blue skies and dreams that come true.

There's just one blanket left.

I thought people would have told Sebastian to stop by now, but they let him continue. Everyone knows what we're doing. Everyone understands that each time we're preparing ourselves for the shock of a familiar face.

And then I see the shoes sticking out from under the third blanket. Big black workman's shoes with scuffed toes.

I look and stagger, but I know there's no one to catch me.

As hard as I can, I press my nails into my palms, and then Sebastian takes off the third blanket.

I don't look at the blood, I only look at the top of the head. There's no hair. The scalp is shiny and bald. Sebastian lays the blanket back.

For the first time since we got out of the taxi, we look at each other.

"Where are they?" I ask hoarsely.

The world no longer feels real. This building with a hole in it was once my school. In the yard strewn with shards of glass, I spent years skipping rope. If you run along the railings with a stick, the metal bars sing.

"Maybe they'd already finished moving stuff," Sebastian says. It's still like looking in a backless mirror. His face is bleached white.

"Maybe they went to buy some buns for Robbie's birthday," I say. "Maybe they're already back in the queue for the Underground."

At that moment, every face in the schoolyard turns to the double doors. Three men slowly emerge from the dark hall. The first two men are carrying a stretcher between them. They're wearing helmets and overalls.

On the stretcher I see a head with a red scarf around it. Knotted on top.

The third man to come outside is Jack.

34

Sebastian has reached the stretcher before they've even put it down.

I go after him but Jack blocks my way.

"Don't look," he says firmly. He takes hold of my arm. "Ella, come with me."

His face is covered in scratches, his lip is fat and he's limping.

"Let me go!" I break free and run to the stretcher.

She's lying there.

A shiver goes down my spine.

It's impossible to hope she's still alive. For the first time in my life, I forbid myself from finding words for what I am seeing. I can't think about the right side of her face. I can't describe the colours. I mustn't describe the shapes. That side is the war side.

The other side of her face is our side.

I look at the cheek that's still smooth, the ear that's still whole, her nose – which is entirely unblemished. Her long dark eyelashes. The lock of hair emerging from under the red headscarf.

Sebastian doesn't make a sound. He sinks to his knees and sits next to his sister. He takes hold of her white fingers, bends his head over her hand and doesn't move from there.

I'm dizzy.

As long as I don't think anything, nothing's definite. As long as I don't cry, I can breathe.

I clench my teeth and sit down next to Sebastian. Jack goes and stands on the other side of him; Robbie kneels on the ground beside me and presses his face into my shoulder.

"I don't want to see," he whispers.

I carry on looking because I can feel her disappearing. These are the last moments. Deep in my brain there are still some dark corners that think she's still alive. I want those corners to stay. I want to keep on waiting forever for the moment she stands on the other side of the street, calling out to me.

For a short while she's still Quinn.

And then it's over.

I see the hole in her head, the blood beginning to congeal.

My mother comes over to us with one of our white sheets. Sebastian slowly stands up. He unfolds the sheet and, in silence, each of us takes hold of a corner: Jack, Robbie, Sebastian and me.

The sheet floats above her for a moment. It bellies out in the wind and then we let it fall.

As soon as the sheet has covered her, Sebastian breaks. We hear him sob; a desperate bellow echoes off the stones. And then he masters himself again.

I look at the sheet and remember Quinn standing in the pouring rain. The way she'd yelled that she didn't want half a life just because she was a girl.

If there was anyone who lived life to the full, it was her.

I shake my head and begin to cry.

35

I tried.

I tried to carry on like everyone else, to spread sandwiches with a stony face.

The fire service is checking whether the damaged school building can still be used; my mother is drumming up other women from the neighbourhood. Big kettles of water need to be heated up so that everyone in the schoolyard can have a cup of tea. Robbie is playing five stones in silence with a group of little children and Sebastian, as pale as a corpse, is having a discussion with two men in helmets. He refuses to let Quinn go.

The three bodies under the dark grey blankets have already been taken to the mortuary. Nobody has said anything about what we all saw: they weren't loaded into a proper hearse but a butcher's van painted grey.

The people who have lost someone sit apart from the rest: the elderly husband of the white-haired lady, the skinny mother of the girl with plaits, the wife and five children of the man with workman's shoes. They stare into space and cry a bit. Nobody does what I want to do: rant and rave and then simply give up.

I'm finding it hard to breathe.

Everyone is busy; everyone is carrying on. Nobody is screaming that she was fifteen and without her it will take much too long to change the world.

I walk away from the sunny schoolyard, around the corner of the building and then around the corner again. I stop in a dark, empty little yard.

My stomach heaves of its own accord. An inhuman sound comes from my throat; my shoulders begin to shake.

There's nobody else so it doesn't matter what this sounds like. I think about Quinn and try to reshape the world.

A world without her.

No hysterical giggles in the rain. No sparkly ideas that make me feel like a window is being opened inside my mind. Nobody to stand up for me, nobody who actually thinks I can write books, nobody who will ever be daring enough to explain to me how a man and a woman fit together.

No new words any more.

I think of the right-hand side of her face and gag.

It's as if I'm seeing what life really is for the first time.

A thing that stops.

But how do you carry on living when you know that we're all going to be destroyed? That one person has to clench their teeth a little longer than another, but that in the end there'll be nothing left of any of us, just a body in a butcher's van?

I cry until I can't cry any more.

I wipe my cheeks, my hands shaking, and I sniff.

And then I turn round and see Jack sitting there.

In the shadows on the ground.

His shirt hangs in tatters around his body; his trousers are torn. He is leaning back against the wall and looking at me. He pats the mossy paving stones next to him without speaking.

I don't know what else to do, so I wipe my nose on my sleeve and sit down next to him.

It's quite a long time before he says anything.

"That bomb in the park was better," he says then. He clears his throat. "It's nicer if you both survive."

Dried-up streams of blood run down his cheeks, his hair is full of plaster dust, his bottom lip is swollen. I remember him limping when he came out of the school building.

"Has anyone checked you over?" I ask. "Shouldn't you go to hospital?"

"What?" He turns his head towards me. "You'll have to talk louder. I can't hear anything in my left ear. The right one is starting to do better…"

His face is very close to my face. I want to repeat what I said but I can't. I see the double doors before me, the dark hall with three figures emerging. First, I saw the stretcher with Quinn, only then did I see Jack.

I wasn't even glad for a second that he'd survived, but now it overwhelms me.

He's still here.

He still exists.

I don't want to be happy because being happy feels like choosing between Quinn and Jack. But I can't do anything about it. A small corner of the dark grey blanket brightens.

I sit there very still. This time I won't move.

And then he moves. He wraps his arms around me. He hugs me tightly without any hesitation, as if this was quite natural. He breathes fast, my cheek touches his neck and I feel his heart beating.

And then it's over. He lets go and doesn't look at me.

"She was so bloody pig-headed!" He balls his fists. "I wanted to take the front of the bench because we were going down the stairs. But she refused. She just wouldn't. I wasn't to treat her like a weakling."

"No one was allowed to carry her suitcase," I say softly.

He doesn't hear me. His eyes are dark in the shadows. "There's a bend in the stairs…"

"I know." Now I'm speaking loudly. "I know the basement. It was my school."

"You went to school here?"

I nod and he wipes his forehead. His hand is covered in scratches too.

"Someone had left a chair on the stairs." He still doesn't look at me. "I dunno which fathead had done that… We were carrying the bench. We went down the stairs and the chair was in the way. And before I could say nothing, Quinn gave it an enormous kick. It flew into the basement and – *boom*."

I lay my hand on his wrist, but as soon as my fingers touch his skin, he pulls his arm away.

"It wasn't a big explosion," he says loudly. "The whole building could've collapsed, hundreds of people buried in the rubble..." He shakes his head. "How crazy is that. A single stray bomb rolls through the basement window at night and doesn't even go off."

I smell the damp basement walls again. I remember that the window was always left open. Sometimes a ball would roll in from the playground and drop down into the basement.

How do you carry on living when you know we're all going to be destroyed?

"Did she say anything?" I whisper. He doesn't hear me. "Did Quinn say anything?" I ask louder.

He shakes his head. "She was dead on impact. I..." He coughs. "I saw her eye – the eye that was still whole – I saw it close. And then I sat down beside her. I thought: They'll come and fetch us at some point. She'll be on her own for long enough after this."

36

I'm standing in the tunnel, and I don't know what to do.

Jack and Robbie are sitting next to each other in silence. They look at the empty spot beside them.

I can't go and sit there. I can't sit still. I'll suffocate if I have to spend the whole night here.

Those first few minutes in the schoolyard felt like the end. There was a white flapping sheet and a translucent blue sky. The world was as clear-cut as a crystal, we were in the exact centre, and nothing could ever be worse than Quinn's half face.

But now it's the evening. The night has already begun, and Quinn is *still dead*.

She'll be dead the whole time for the rest of my life. It's unbearable.

"It should have been me," I say decisively. "In the iron lung, or that night in the park. I should have been the one to die."

"You can't pick who kicks the bucket," Jack says calmly.

"Why not?" I cry. "How do people cope when it's so *unfair*!" My voice bounces off the tunnel walls. "I've got pain all the time and I'll have to live with my parents for the rest of my life. It should've been me!"

"Don't be so stupid." He wipes his hair back off his forehead in irritation. "Who says Quinn will be the only one? Maybe a bomb will fall on this station tonight. Maybe you'll get run over by a bus tomorrow. Maybe I'll get shot down two years from now. It's a war. Did you really think everybody would survive?"

"Wow," says Robbie. "You're really good at comforting people."

I say nothing.

Jack sits up a little. I see him clenching his teeth as he moves his leg. He can hear again with his right ear, but there's a squeal in his left one.

Before we came to the tunnel, he washed himself in our kitchen. I boiled a kettle of water, gave him a clean towel and went upstairs to look for one of my father's shirts. After that, I got Quinn's suitcase out from under my bed. I didn't open it, I just rested my hands on the leather. I stayed there, quietly waiting like that.

And now I'm back in the tunnel. "Sebastian's family is acting like he doesn't exist," I say without looking at them. "They've erased him from their lives. But tomorrow he'll have to go home."

This is the last night that Quinn's body will be in London. I look at the blocked end of the tunnel. A wall with nothing but dark soil behind it.

"I keep picturing it. Sebastian driving through these big gates, past stone columns with lions on them, and his parents come out. They stand on the doorstep of their country mansion and look at their son. And then he'll have to tell them what happened. The world has changed while they've been playing tennis and drinking tea. And now it's too late for all the things they wanted to say to each other."

I keep my eyes fixed on the end of the tunnel, all that earth to bury people in. And then I hear Jack sigh.

"I'm picturing it too. They're lucky Sebastian's stopped wearing that dressing gown."

"You're still an idiot."

"I know." He shrugs. "I'm not used to talking about dead people. When my ma kicked the bucket, Dad never said another word about her again. Easier that way. Less room for bad jokes."

I want to wrap my arms around him and then give him a smack. Or the other way around.

"She wanted to tell her parents about her life here," I say. "She even wanted to tell them about us."

He raises his eyebrows. "But she hated her folks, didn't she?"

"She hated their ideas." I look at him. "Do you know she really did have a title? Her father's a lord, so Quinn was a lady..."

He whistles softly. "Then they're gonna be thrilled when Sebastian fills them in. They won't believe the kind of company their daughter's been keeping in London."

"A plunderer," I say. "An invalid. And a street urchin..."

I think of the first time I saw her. A film star in men's trousers on her way to be a nurse.

From the first moment she acted like it was normal for us to be talking to each other. She worried if we had enough porridge for her, but she saw more than just my leg, more than my outgrown dress.

She saw *me.*

"I hope they don't open the coffin," Robbie says. "I hope Sebastian tells them it's better not to look."

A shiver runs down my back. Even with a jumper and a cardigan, I'm cold.

Jack turns the worn heel of his shoe in the dirt. "When I was finally allowed home, my ma was already gone. I was furious."

"Quinn had a row before she left," Robbie says. "They haven't seen her for three weeks. They don't know anything about her life here and now she's dead."

"Enough!" I cry. I'm finding it hard to stay standing, but I refuse to sit down. "Jack was right. There's no use talking about it. Do you think the noble lord and lady would want to know their daughter scrubbed floors? That she had dirty nails and she was still happy?"

"Yes," Jack says. "I reckon they would."

"What?" I'm confused.

"I think they'd want the chance to hear what Quinn had to say." He looks at me. "We were there. We know what she wanted to say."

My heart begins to pound.

"We know her stories," Jack says.

"I'm not going to them," I cry. I take a step back. "Those people are blind. You know what they'd see if we turned up on their doorstep."

He nods. "A plunderer and an invalid. I'm not thinking about going to see them. We don't need to. You could just write it down."

My legs nearly give way.

Suddenly, I'm reminded of the last war, when countless thousands of men died in the trenches. The spring after that, Flanders' fields were covered in poppies.

At school we read a poem about those fields full of graves and blood-red poppies. It never occurred to me as I memorised that poem that we should stop talking about what happened.

"I can't just write about Quinn…"

"Why not? You know all the letters!"

"That's not enough for a story."

"It ain't a story," Jack says. "It's her life."

Without wanting to, I imagine the notebook on my knees. I feel the pencil between my fingers; I feel how clear my mind becomes when it's allowed to think about words on paper.

"About the three of us too?" I ask.

"Yeah. Let people see that we're more than nameless poor beggars."

"I can't remember everything," I whisper.

"We'll help you," Robbie says.

37

We climb up on to the platform. We need some supplies. Candles, extra paper, preferably some extra food too if we're going to stay awake all night.

The lord and lady will probably think differently but we're not beggars. I've never in my life asked anyone who wasn't part of my family for anything. Jack hasn't either – he turns a few tricks or just takes what he wants.

But today we walk along the platform asking people to help us. They've barely anything themselves and everyone's wondering how long we're going to have to put on a brave face for. And still they give us all kinds of things: a handful of raisins, an empty paper bag to write on, a few matches, a candle stub.

They hear what we want to do, and about this, every one of them is certain: people need to talk about the dead. However many there are, however long this goes on for, however tired we get.

If we start acting like life has no value, then life starts not to have any value.

They look at me with a respect I've never known before.

"Write it down," they say. "This mustn't be forgotten."

I can't give a reply, I just nod. And despite it all, something deep inside begins to shine.

When we've gathered enough supplies, we go back to the tunnel. I get out my grey notebook and tear out all the pages that have been written on. Quinn's life is going to go on the empty pages that are left. But first I take the paper bag to make some notes.

"Tell me," I say, sitting in between Jack and Robbie. "Tell me everything you remember."

"I was the first to see her." Jack takes a bite of an apple we got from a man with so few teeth it made you wonder how he could have eaten it anyway. "She got off the train in those funny trousers of hers and looked around."

"How did she seem? Her expression?" I ask. "I need to know."

He thinks. "She had a face like she was about to eat a whole apple pie in one go."

"That's not a face!"

"It was on her."

I note down: *Arrival at station – whole apple pie.*

"The first time I saw her was when you fainted," Robbie says. "First, she helped carry you, then she ran off. She almost dropped you on the platform! But luckily Jack had a good grip…"

I say nothing but Jack begins to chuckle. "And then my expression was like I had to carry a whole invalid on my own."

"You don't get similes at all," I snap. I lick my pencil. "Carry on."

"The second time I saw her," Jack says, "you were there too. The both of you looking for her case in Old William's stinking cavern, and she was having the time of her life. That's when I knew she was fearless. There was nothing she wouldn't dare do."

"She taught me three different card games," Robbie says. "Her dad's brilliant at cards and when she was little he let her win sometimes. She said she was so proud when he stopped doing that."

"She was strict." Jack sighs. "She had no patience for people who mess around."

I nod. "The world won't change if people keep messing around."

"She made sure I could sleep in the tunnel with you," says Robbie. "She talked to me like I was important."

The paper bag rests on my knees; the flames of two candles flicker. When my pencil gets blunt, Jack sharpens it with his penknife. We drink borrowed tea, we eat the raisins people gave us because they want me to be able to carry on, and for the first time in my life, words are not an escape.

They are what remains.

And then Robbie and Jack have told me everything they remember. On the paper bag there's a long list, but the list in my head is even longer.

Now I have to start.

I open the notebook and suddenly it overwhelms me. Tomorrow morning, when Sebastian comes to collect Quinn's suitcase from our house, I'll give him the notebook.

Later, in their chilly country manor, the lord and lady will read this. They'll learn about their daughter's final weeks through my words.

If I write that Quinn looked like she was about to eat a whole apple pie, that's the way they'll picture her. They're rich and descended from William the Conqueror, but I'm choosing the words. A pencil and paper are enough.

I begin to write.

They have to know everything: that the pavement was made of rubber when she walked next to me; that she was *so* full of life I found it hard to watch at times; that she thought the Underground was the name of a hotel; that it mattered that she existed.

38

It's three in the morning and I'm still far from the end. My wrist hurts, my arm has cramp, my fingers shake when I stop writing. So I carry on.

Robbie fell asleep a long time ago. I've told Jack to sleep too. Today he survived a UXB – he must be shattered. But he doesn't sleep. He sits next to me, sometimes sets down a new candle stub, pours me a mug of tea and sharpens my pencil.

"Where've you got to now?" he asks as he passes me a slice of currant loaf.

I take a big bite. "The bit where she told me she misses her parents."

"Read it out, will you?"

"It's not for reading out loud."

He closes his penknife. And then opens it again. The metal glints in the candlelight. "Can I hear it anyway?"

"So that you can crack jokes about it?"

"Of course," he says immediately. And then he shrugs. "You always listen to everyone. I dunno how you do it, but people always tell you everything. Now I wanna hear you talk."

He looks me in the eye and that very first day flashes through my mind. I was in the queue for the Underground, and he looked at me. For an instant, I thought he saw more than the rest.

I clear my throat and begin to read. Two paragraphs and then I stop.

He closes his knife again. "And now about that night in the park."

My fingers begin to tingle.

"I'm not writing about that," I say without looking at him. "I'm writing about Quinn. She wasn't there, that night in the park."

He's quiet for a moment, and then he says seriously, "I looked like I'd just been given a whole ham."

"What?!" I stare at him.

"You keep asking what people looked like? Well, like that. When you kissed me, I looked like I'd just been given a whole ham."

I shake my head. "You still don't get similes! If someone suddenly gives you a whole ham, you look *happy*!"

"Exactly. That's what I mean."

He's quiet, and the tunnel fills with sparks.

I clear my throat. "Are all your similes about food?"

He begins to chuckle. "I don't know what a simile is, but think about it!" He points to the book on my knees. "This story takes place in a war. What would anyone today be pleased as punch with? Well, if you suddenly got a whole ham without having to queue, without having to pay with money and coupons…"

He keeps looking at me, and suddenly nothing in the world seems as romantic as *a whole ham*.

"I have a limp," I say.

He frowns. "That's not a simile, is it?"

"No, it's a fact. And it'll never go away."

"Does having a limp mean you can't eat ham?" he asks calmly.

"Shut up about ham," I say. And then I hesitate. "If you have a limp…other people probably don't want to eat ham with you."

"All right," he says. "Now *I've* had enough. Shut up about that ham!"

I don't say anything else. The candle between us has gone out.

"Cards on the table," he says suddenly.

"What do you mean?" I ask in surprise.

"I'm penniless. I can't promise you anything. If we kiss now, that'll make me a scoundrel and you a—"

It feels like flares are coming down on parachutes again. As though planes are roaring deep in my belly.

"Good," I interrupt.

He shakes his head. "You don't get it! You're fourteen. And I know you're a respectable girl. You don't want people talking about you, do you?"

I sit there very quietly in the semi-darkness.

I think back to this morning at the zoo, my conversation with Sebastian. I couldn't imagine what it must be like to have other people always decide what you can and can't do with your body. I told Sebastian he had to fight. And he'd looked at me and asked: *Is that what you do?*

"Quinn didn't live her life the way things are," I say to Jack. "She lived the way things should be. She didn't wait until everyone else changed the world. She went about it herself."

I put my hand around the back of his neck, pull his face towards me and kiss him.

This time I don't stop. And this time he kisses back.

It's unbelievable. I feel his arms around me, his breath on my face, his tongue in my mouth – and I'm not even thinking about being sent into quarantine.

We've stopped talking. He doesn't make any more jokes. We're doing something together that is completely serious and at the same time cheerful. We smile when our noses bump; our breathing becomes heavier. I press myself to him in a dizzying combination of touching and being touched, wanting and being wanted.

It feels like hunger. It feels like our lives depend on it. It feels unimaginable that we lost so much time while all those weeks our bodies were already here.

And then we stop and look at each other, out of breath.

He studies every detail of my face, and I don't look away. I can see it now. It does matter to him that I exist.

39

The platform guard's voice echoes through the tunnel. "All clear! Please leave the station!"

A new day is beginning.

Robbie sits up, rubs his eyes and looks at Jack and me. We're sitting between the girders on the other side; we didn't want to wake him.

"Did you manage it?" my brother asks. "Did you write it all down?"

"Yes," I say, and my voice sounds different from yesterday.

"Did you get any sleep?"

"Nah," Jack says in a serious voice. "There wasn't any time to sleep."

It feels as though we're still touching each other. I know this feeling will pass, that he'll disappear for the whole day, that he's into wheeling and dealing and that he hasn't promised me anything.

But he did promise he'll come back to the tunnel tonight.

"And?" Robbie points at the grey book. "How does the story end?"

Jack raises his eyebrows. "She dies. Did you miss that yesterday?"

"I mean with us," Robbie says quietly.

I gulp. He's only just turned ten and he didn't want to look at Quinn. But she was there. She lay there in the schoolyard, and it was impossible not to see her.

The air raids have only recently begun but the schools have been shut for over a year. What's to become of Robbie? How long will it be before he's forgotten how to read too?

At the end of the war, will he still look away when he sees a broken body?

I look at the notebook and think about last night. Not those last hours with Jack but the start. As I sat there writing, I felt it happening: for a brief instant, Quinn came back to life.

I'll never forget anything about last night.

My whole life long.

I choose the words.

"You," I say to Robbie, "are going to be the manager of the zoo." I take a deep breath. "You'll start as an assistant in the monkey enclosure. For years you'll only be allowed to clean cages and repair fences. But then they'll see what you're capable of. And you'll become the manager."

Robbie looks serious. "That's good." And then he begins to giggle. "Jack ends up behind bars, of course."

"Undoubtedly," Jack says immediately. He looks at me. "You'll sail to America and write books."

I hold my breath. "About what?"

"A new world."

He smiles at me, and I feel our hunger from the night again.

"Let me know which prison you're in," I say. "I'll send you my books."

"Will I be able to read them?"

I nod. "I'll have spent the whole war teaching you to read."

We look at each and I know we're thinking about things that don't have much to do with the difference between a B and a D.

"And Sebastian then?" Robbie asks. "He'll have to join the army next summer…"

I clasp my hands.

In a couple of hours' time, he'll be at our door to collect Quinn's case. I'll give him the grey notebook and he'll leave. He's a toff. He's rich and Quinn's gone. I've no idea whether we'll ever see him again after that.

"Sebastian will be there when they free Europe," I say softly. "The day the war ends, people everywhere will go outside. They'll start to dance in the street and Sebastian will walk through the dancing people in his uniform. And then he'll fall in love."

Robbie begins to giggle. "Who with?"

"One of the dancing people. And then he'll stay there. In a land or a city or a house without cages."

Jack gets up. "We've got to go."

I fold up my flowery bedspread. Jack pulls on a jumper he found at Old William's and Robbie pats the dust from his new blazer.

Yesterday it was his birthday. Quinn has only been dead for a day.

Before we leave, we pause, the three of us, just a while in front of her place between the girders. And then we leave.

As we slowly walk along the platform, I hear in my head the song Sebastian sang a week ago.

We'll meet again,
Don't know where,
Don't know when,
But I know we'll meet again some sunny day…

In silence, hundreds of people put on their jackets and shoes. They load up their carts and shake their blankets over the tracks even though there are posters everywhere saying that it is strictly forbidden to shake out the fleas from your bedding in the Underground.

Another night has passed. Our station is still standing; we stream up the escalators. Thousands of ordinary people have survived another little bit of the war. They walk up the last steps into the daylight. In the grey morning there's a van where you can buy tea, coffee and soup. Everyone's got used to spending each night sheltering here.

I stand on the pavement where it all began and look up. The sun glitters in the highest windows.

Finally: six years later

I stand at the railing and this time it's real. The enormous ship sighs as it heaves on the waves; the grey ocean is endless and beyond the horizon is a new life.

I'm twenty.

I still have a limp. I'm a little less skinny. My hair's still mousy, but I no longer care.

The war is over.

We sheltered under the ground for longer than we ever thought possible. England was bombed for more than eight months in a row.

The Blitz continued until May 1941. It didn't stop because the war was over but because Hitler needed his planes elsewhere. The war roared on, but for us in England, the bombing stopped for a while.

It was a cold, wet spring. We went outside, looked around and then it really hit us. For eight months and five days we'd held our breath. For more than eight months, we didn't spend a single night in our own beds, hurrying every morning through the quiet streets to check whether our homes were still standing.

We'd celebrated Christmas under the ground, with decorated trees and carols on the platform. The government set up bunk beds and chemical toilets; the Underground was hung with posters listing rules and regulations to make the madness more manageable.

All that time we'd carried on blindly, waiting and hoping. And when it stopped, hundreds of thousands of homes had been destroyed and tens of thousands of lives lost.

I clutch the railing with my hands and breathe in the salty air. There's no land in sight; the sea pounds. I'm a tiny little dot in the ocean.

We made it through.

After Sebastian left with the grey notebook, we didn't hear anything for seven weeks. Then a heavy parcel was delivered to our house. It was for me. There was an envelope stuck to it with my name on, and in that envelope there was a card that said two words:

Thank you.

I pulled the string loose, tore open the paper, and right then I realised that the lord and lady were not made of stone. I've never seen them in real life. They never came to visit us. But somewhere deep under the waves, in the hold of this ship, they're safe in my cabin trunk: Quinn's dictionaries. The world in twelve dark blue volumes.

They gave me her words.

Around me, men and women with babies stand at the railing. Scarves flap; children laugh. I look silently at the foaming water and think about all the people I've left behind.

And then I feel two hands around my waist. I don't look, I simply begin to smile. I know his arms better than my own, his eyes that are the colour of barrage balloons.

"Are you coming in?" Jack asks.

He was called up when he turned eighteen. He went and I stayed behind. He hadn't promised me anything. It was another three years until the war was over. And then he came back and promised me everything. A new world. A new life.

So now we're on our way there.

The sea breeze fills my lungs. I feel Jack's arms around me, his lips close to my ear.

"Come back to our cabin!"

"Yes," I say, because I want to know what's going to happen next.

And tomorrow. And after that.

1
2
3
4

5
6
7
8

Photo Credits

Page 212:

1. Families in London sleep underground to shelter from the bombs in Aldwych tube station, 1940.
2. A woman carries what's left of her belongings in a cart while talking to an Air Raids Precautions worker. London, 1940.
3. Several railway stations were damaged during the Blitz. This one in Westminster Bridge Road was hit during London's biggest night raid of the war, on 16 April 1941.
4. A German Heinkel 111 bomber flies over the River Thames and Tower Bridge in London, taken on 7 September 1940.

Page 213:

5. The night raids caused countless fires and turned many buildings into rubble. Here, firefighters work among burnt-out buildings in Ludgate Hill.
6. Tower Bridge stands out against the smoke billowing across London, taken after the first mass German air raid against Britain.
7. A dedicated aircraft spotter stands on a roof and searches the skies for enemy planes with his binoculars, with St Paul's Cathedral in the background.
8. Brave firefighters work to put out the raging fires caused by the bombings.

Source:

Photo 1: CBW/Alamy Stock Photo; Photos 2–8: Everett Collection/ Shutterstock.com.

TEN FACTS ABOUT THE BLITZ

1. The term "Blitz" comes from the German *Blitzkrieg*, meaning "Lightning War".

2. London was the main target. The first air raid was on 7 September 1940 – a day known as "Black Saturday". The bombing continued for fifty-seven consecutive nights.

3. The densely populated East End of London and its docks were frequent targets. The aim was to disrupt the supply of food and goods entering the port.

4. The Blitz lasted for eight months, until 11 May 1941, and resulted in more than 43,500 civilian deaths. Many more were injured or left homeless.

5. The bombing also damaged the Houses of Parliament, Buckingham Palace and the Tower of London. Luckily, St Paul's Cathedral was left unscathed. It became a symbol of London's survival.

6. On 14 October 1940, tragedy struck at Balham Underground station. A night-time bomb caused a huge crater and ruptured a water main, flooding the station and killing nearly seventy people.

7. As more people took to sleeping in the Underground, more facilities were put in place. Toilets were built, performances and evening classes were held and there was even the "Tube Refreshments Special", a train service that delivered food and drink to those sheltering on the platforms.

8. Coventry, Birmingham and Liverpool also faced significant bombings due to the key roles they played in producing war materials. More than half of the houses in Coventry were damaged or destroyed on 14 November 1940.

9. The Blitz led to an increase in crime. Many police officers left to become soldiers, while the nightly blackouts and the desperation caused by food and clothing rations meant some people saw it as a perfect opportunity to loot damaged homes and shops.

10. Britain retaliated with bombing campaigns abroad, also targeting civilians. In Hamburg, Germany, a week of British bombing raids in 1943 killed around 40,000 people.

© Carli Hermès

Anna Woltz is an internationally bestselling children's author based in the Netherlands. She studied History because the past is full of amazing stories. Anna has written twenty-nine books, which have been translated into thirty languages and won numerous prizes. *Under the London Sky* won the Dutch Zilveren Griffel and the German Gustav Heinemann Peace Award.

© Jagoda Lasota

Michele Hutchison is a multi-award-winning translator based in the Netherlands. She has translated many Dutch novels including the winner of the 2020 International Booker prize, *The Discomfort of Evening* by Lucas Rijneveld. Other works include *Stage Four* by Sander Kollaard and *We Are Light* by Gerda Blees. Her two children grew up reading and loving Anna Woltz's novels in the original Dutch.